"I'm impetuous—always have been . . ."

she confessed to the captain. "So it breeds trouble? Well, charge on and find some more trouble, I say. I suppose if one wants to spend one's life adventuring, it's a handy trait to have. But it does cause wear and tear and pain."

"I admire immensely your gift for plunging ahead and burning your bridges behind you." His compliment sounded sincere. "I should be more impulsive," he admitted. "I'm too cautious, too slow at times."

"And I must learn to take better heed," she continued. "You're a very good model for me. You're steady. You're proper and careful, and it is glaringly obvious that I am not. And, of course, there's that matter of impulsiveness."

"Impulsiveness. Yes." He was drawing her head toward his. It took her a moment to realize what was coming. Somehow she could easily picture Maude kissing just any old pair of lips that wandered into range—but this was different, very different.

Their lips met softly. He wrapped around her, encased her in the strength of his arms. Her body, her spirit, all her senses hung suspended. How long did she float in this happy oblivion? In due time his lips left hers, brushed along her cheek, burrowed in her neck. His hand pressed her head against his shoulder.

"Excellent impulse. You learn quickly," she murmured.

"Not impulse. That action was very carefully considered."

She drew away a little. "Uh, Captain . . . If your God is looking over your shoulder just now, as you say He often does, would He approve of me?"

SONG
OF THE
NEREIDS

Sandy Dengler

Serenade/Saga
BOOKS

of the Zondervan Publishing House
Grand Rapids, Michigan

Other Serenade/ Saga Books by Sandy Dengler

Summer Snow

SONG OF THE NEREIDS
Copyright © 1984 by The Zondervan Corporation
Grand Rapids, Michigan

ISBN 0-310-46472-2

Edited by Anne Severance and Nancye Willis

Designed by Kim Koning

Printed in the United States of America

84 85 86 87 88 / 10 9 8 7 6 5 4 3 2 1

THE BEGINNING OF AN ADVENTURE . . . .

Singapore, Dusk, June 7, 1851

She despised rain. She despised warm rain even more, and no other kind of rain ever fell on Singapore. She despised Singapore, most of all, this waterfront. She ambled slowly along the pier. Rain rivulets ran down the planking to disappear in cracks between the boards. Boats flopped listlessly at their moorings. The wet air hung heavy with a hundred odors, every one of them foul. All the bustling city's waste flushed itself down here to the docks. A carabao swayed past her dragging a creaky wooden cart. Its half-sweet bovine smell added itself to all the other smells.

Two years ago in Chelsea, distant Chelsea, she had yearned to see exotic places and go adventuring. She had dreamt of warm tropical climes. The irony of it almost tickled her funny bone, though there was surely no real humor in the thought.

Above the constant rustle of rain a sailor shouted in English. Another answered. A bark of moderate size was just now tying up a few hundred feet ahead. Its flaccid sails drooped wet from their spars. Soaked and disspirited, the

Union Jack hung near the mizzen. *British ship. Home.*

Mooring hawsers thunked against the pier planks. She was constantly amazed by the sheer size of the ropes on ships. A section of the starboard railing opened; a gangplank was thrown out. It dropped—*kunnng*—against the pier. More shouting. Men docking a ship were much like hens laying eggs; neither could perform quietly.

She pulled her shawl closer around her head, but it offered scant protection against the rain. A lock of her hair plastered itself against her cheek—all sticky. It would soon be dark. She had best start back.

From the bark, a voice with a distinctive Scots brogue called, "God bless the lad, sir!"

A man wearing a black jacket and carrying a large bundle jogged down the plank. Two small, bare feet dangled from one end of the bundle and the man clutched the other end close to his shoulder. *A sick child?* It looked so. The man was walking rapidly, almost at a dog trot, directly toward her. She shrank back into the shadows too late. He obviously had seen her.

He paused right in front of her. "Can you tell me where I can find a doctor?"

His bundle was indeed a sick child. The little boy's face, normally weather-tanned, was flushed. Even in this half-light she could see ragged brown fever lines across his lips.

"A doctor? Yes. Go three—uh, leave the waterfront at that gray building and go north—" She shook her head. "Let me take you."

"I'm grateful. Thank-you." He fell in behind her as she turned on her heel and hurried off.

No matter how brisk her step, he kept up easily. Her back was to him, but his face haunted her nonetheless. He was a rather handsome fellow. No doubt he had a girl in every port and only a few of them his wives. He was well built, but

6

then most seamen were well built. He had dark hair, but everyone in Singapore had dark hair except herself; her's was a warm brown. Tanned skin like his was common enough. It must be the eyes that moved her so. They were warm and dark, the largest eyes she had ever seen in a man—deep reservoirs of fear and worry. Was the boy his son? A cabin boy? A shaver? A total stranger?

She panted from the exertion. Barely twenty years old, she felt like sixty. Although he was only medium sized, as men go, she was petite enough that her head barely reached his shoulder. No wonder he so easily outpaced her. His long legs were taking two strides to her three. Salty sweat mixed with the rain on her face.

She felt confident, leading him to the British sector. Even if he were familiar with this part of Singapore he'd never find the right street and door.

Some of the more noxious odors had been left behind. They turned here at the chicken-seller's deserted stall. The fourth door on the left—here they were.

"This door right here. I assumed you'd want an English doctor rather than Chinese." She jogged up the wooden stoop and pounded the knocker up and down for him, since his arms were full.

He stared absently at the door knocker. The knocker, a brass lion with a ring in its mouth, stared absently back at him. Sun crinkles in the corners of his eyes etched deeply, as did the worry frown across his forehead. She wished she could watch his face when he was jovial. She could just imagine the sun crinkles bunching up as he laughed. How old was he? Thirty-five at the most, and probably not quite that.

The door swung open. A Chinese houseman stood in the gloom. "Yes?"

"Captain Travis Bricker. My cabin boy here requires a

doctor's attention immediately. He is very ill."

The man bowed elegantly. "Come in, Captain."

Captain Bricker stepped inside and followed the house-man down the long dark hall.

She had done her good deed. She should leave now. Instead she found herself following that jacket down the hall. She was sworn off men. She was through with the fickle animals. Why did this one fascinate her so? At the houseman's direction the captain laid his burden on a waist-high teak table and unwrapped the blanket.

Moments later the doctor appeared through a side door. A rotund man with muttonchop whiskers, he had to lean quite a bit to bend over his examination table. He slipped a stethoscope into his ears and studied the ceiling as he listened to this part and that of the lad. She hung back in the doorway watching.

The doctor grunted. "What medicines has he received today?"

"None. We tried to control his fever with quinine and the convulsions with laudanum, but we ran out of both two days ago."

"The proper medications. His fever waxes and wanes, so to speak?"

"Yes."

The doctor grunted and nodded again.

The captain stepped away from the table, stretched his back and rubbed his face with both hands. No doubt part of the sadness in his face was simply a lack of sleep.

"Your cabin boy, I presume. He receives good nourishment?"

"My cabin boy, yes. And he eats like any two seamen before the mast. His appetite matches Edward's, helping for helping." He sighed heavily. "Edward was cabin boy when this voyage began, but he's really too old for the work. He wanted to sail before the mast and I gladly signed him on as a seaman. I suppose if I can't find another cabin boy, I'll have to put Edward back in the stern again. I trust Gideon here won't be able to take up duties for a long time."

"Several months. In fact, he shouldn't be asea, assuming he lives."

"Leave him here?"

"I recommend it."

The captain paced about, rubbing the back of his neck. "We're due to meet a buyer; I diverted to bring Gideon here; can't lose much more time—" His voice trailed away.

She pondered the voice. He was not English, Aussie, or Canadian, yet there was somehow a touch of the Canadian accent.

"Very well. I have friends here where Gideon can stay awhile. And I'll just have to put Edward to serving again."

A brilliant idea dawned so suddenly it startled her. "Sir? Captain?"

He looked at her for the first time. "I'm so very sorry, Miss! Not only have I neglected to thank you, I've ignored you. Please accept my apology. I couldn't have found this place without you. How can I repay?" He was reaching into an inner jacket pocket.

She held up her hand. "Please, no. You're most freely welcome, sir. But I was just thinking: my brother is seeking work. He's younger than I, but too old to apprentice. And there are precious few jobs for a white boy in Singapore. He's never been to sea but he's accustomed to serving and he learns quickly. Might you consider him as cabin boy, please?"

"I'll be glad to talk to him. Send him around tomorrow morning. You know where we're berthed. The *Arachne*."

"Thank-you. He'll be most pleased to hear about this." She hesitated. "You're an American?"

He smiled suddenly. Those sun crinkles did indeed bunch up, and in a most delightful way. "Yes. Millinocket, Maine. I may be doubly indebted to you if I can use him. What's his name?"

"Eric Rollin. Shall I tell him to bring anything?"

"References from other employers if he has them. And your name?"

"Margaret Rollin Rice. Good evening, Captain Bricker."

"Good evening. Thank-you again very much, Mrs. Rice."

The houseman bowed curtly and led her to the door. She walked the cool, dark hall, and paused as the houseman opened the outside door. She stepped into the warm and stinking night rain.

She despised Singapore.

CHAPTER 1

Singapore waterfront, Morning, June 8, 1851

The rain was ended, the early morning mist lifting. Travis Bricker appreciated the way this weather reflected his own good mood—improved, much improved, even say bright. Mist no longer muffled noise. His heels rapped hollowly on the boardwalk. The cacophony of a hundred native entrepreneurs hawking everything from chickens to finch cages was constant. Trapped between pier and lolling hulls, the murky water sloshed back and forth. He came abreast *Arachne* and strode up the gangway. It felt good to be home.

"Top o' the morning, sir!" lilted a familiar voice from the quarterdeck.

Bricker stopped by the mizzen to wait. Seamus Fisher tucked the sextant under his arm and came bounding down the starboard steps. *Should a more ebullent Irishman ever be born,* Bricker mused, *Bosun Fisher would still outbounce him!*

The cheery redhead brandished a slip of paper. "Ye'll be pleased to 'ear, sir, that Singapore sits precisely upon the coordinates touted for it. Not only is y'r chronometer in fine mettle, whatever ye did to the sextant corrected that problem as well.''

"Excellent. It'll be nice to know where we are again."

Fisher followed him to the stern cabin door. "I can tell by y'r sprightly demeanor, sir, that the lad is faring well.''

"Doctor broke his fever last night. But he's too weak for sea duty. I'm going to ask Wang See if there's someone he can live with awhile. Given rest and good food he should be back to his usual high level of impishness in a few months. Is Mr. McGovern about?''

"Aye, and the candidate for y'r new cabin boy, sir.'' Fisher leaned forward and pushed the cabin door open.

"Already?'' Bricker stepped from muggy brightness to cool darkness and paused a moment until his eyes adjusted. He nodded toward his first mate. "Good morning, Mr. McGovern.''

"Morning, sir!'' The dour Scot never laughed uproariously, rarely laughed at all, and seldom smiled. He was smiling now. "Our lad's on the mend, aye?''

"Aye. And you must be Eric Rollin,'' he said as a mere wisp of a lad bolted to his feet.

"Yes, sir. I mean, aye, sir.'' He crunched his cap together in his hands and stood tensely, nervously, like a slave being inspected by a prospective buyer. Somehow Bricker had expected a larger boy than this, though size was surely no requirement for the position. And yet the boy seemed poised despite his nervousness, self-confident. His coppery brown hair, undisciplined, flew away all over his head; he needed a proper haircut. And his clothes fitted badly. But those blue eyes sparkled with the same mischievous twinkle that had rendered young Gideon so endearing. Bricker liked the boy instantly.

Bricker wandered over and flopped down in his favorite

chair. He was so tired he ached. "Tell me about yourself, lad."

The boy licked his lips. "Our parents were missionaries in the Far East here. Uh, God took them home untimely. You've met my sister; she married locally. But I wish to return to our native England to complete my schooling, though I'm in no hurry for that, I assure you, sir. I'll not jump ship the moment I see a white face and leave you in want. Nothing of that sort. I'll serve you well, sir. But England's my eventual goal."

"A worthy goal. Any prior experience?"

"None in this line, sir. I've no letters of reference. I serve my sister's and her husband's household. She taught me; they both did. For whatever it's worth, sir, my sister claims I'm quick to learn. She says it's never a waste to know a good line of work, whether I return to school or not."

"Divinity school? You mentioned your parents were missionaries."

"I've not decided, sir. Time enough for that, I'm told."

"True. You seem more mature than your size would suggest."

"Small for my age, sir. My brother-in-law assures me I'm just slow getting my growth. Hope he's right." The boy's big blue eyes met Bricker's squarely, hopefully, as if there were no doubt at all that he would make an absolutely splendid cabin boy.

Bricker glanced over at his first mate. McGovern gave the barest of affirmative nods. An accolade.

"Long months at sea, tedious work, scant pay, rough weather. Certain you want to do this?"

"Positive! Aye, sir!" He smiled warmly, broadly, expectantly.

"I certainly can't fault your enthusiasm, or your motives. The desire for an education is laudable." Bricker hauled to his feet and stretched. "Very well. Fetch your duffle aboard promptly. Yours is that closet there. I'll make arrangement for Gideon's keep this morning and return by noon, Lord willing. We sail right after the noontime meal.

The boy snapped a perky little bow. "I'll be back directly, sir. I thank-you very much for this opportunity. I promise I'll do my best to serve you well."

"I can't ask for more." Bricker started for the door. The boy darted ahead to hold it for him.

Bricker stepped into full-blown tropical sun. It burned his weary eyes but did not obliterate the approaching vision. The Scotsman grunted into Bricker's left ear in surprise, then whispered coarsely, "I smell money boarding, sir."

Bricker had never seen a waistline so slim, or a bustline so artfully sculptured. The woman's dress was the essence of European high fashion. Three or four acres of vivid blue silk swirled down over her crinolines. Draped silk, ruffles, and laces highlighted all the best parts of her form. Even the obligatory shawl was appropriate to this heat, a pale blue swath of some sort of see-through fabric. It draped her bare shoulders elegantly to blend with the silk of her sleeves. Her dainty bonnet and ringlets of dark hair completed the picture of perfection.

She did not walk. She glided, the silk rustling delicately with each dainty step. She paused and looked right at him with liquid brown eyes. "The captain, please." Her tone of voice intimated strongly that she owned this vessel, though Bricker distinctly remembered being responsible to two owners in London.

"I'm the captain, Travis Bricker. Your servant, madam. How can we help you?" He dipped his head.

Were a man to look him over as she looked him over now, he would have been angered by the air of cold disdain. Somehow in her he didn't mind it.

"Maude Harrington. Miss Harrington. I require passage to the East Coast of the United States, preferably the New York area. I understand you're going that way."

"Possibly, but not by a direct route. I have promise of cargo in New Zealand if I arrive there in time, but we'll be sailing contrary to the prevailing winds. We may call at Valparaiso before heading east around the Horn. The voyage will take the better part of a year."

"Very well. Then from New Zealand you'll sail north to Honolulu and San Francisco. The West Coast will do."

Bricker felt the hairs on his neck bristle a bit. "With all respect, madam, you'll not reach the West Coast aboard this vessel. Gold fever is hot in California. Were I to touch the coast there, half my seamen would change their occupation to gold miner and leave me with no crew. A hundred and fifty vessels lie rotting in San Francisco Bay right now for lack of a crew, and *Arachne* will not become one of them."

"You're overly cautious, Captain. Ships call at San Francisco constantly without being stuck there. Shall we say San Diego? Inconvenient, but I'll put up with the extra travel. Provided the Pacific passage is satisfactory. Book me to San Diego."

"No, madam." Bricker folded his arms. He tried to keep her obvious and lovely attributes from distracting him so. "I can put you ashore at Callao, in Peru. Or Panama. I understand gold seekers by the hundreds are pouring across the isthmus to avoid the Horn. There should be guides aplenty to lead you safely to the Atlantic side, and from there ships to take you anywhere you wish to go."

Her eyes snapped. "I can just see myself standing on some desolate Panamanian beach, where eager natives will crowd about simply overjoyed to help me," she said, with scathing sarcasm. "Surely you know Panama is in a state of rebellion. Between Panama's rebels and Colombia's regulars, I'd be in a pretty fix indeed. You will take me to America directly."

"I will not."

"Don't ever call yourself a gentleman where I can hear you, Captain. I shall book passage to New Zealand and make other arrangements from there. When do we sail?"

"Immediately. Will that be soon enough?"

How could such rich, dark eyes be so ice cold? "I've never really appreciated the Yankee sense of humor, such as it is. Your sardonic wit is wasted on me, Captain, and best not offered at all. A carriage will be by with my trunks." She adjusted her mouth into a cold and unfeeling smile. "Thank-you, Captain, and good day." All swishes and swirls, she flounced down the gangway. The dark pipe curls bobbed beneath the bonnet as the smooth, milk-white shoulders disappeared from view.

"Is a cabin boy permitted to voice an opinion, sir?"

"Only when asked to do so." Bricker glanced down at the lad, bemused. "And what is your opinion?"

"Charge her twice the fare, sir, for you'll earn every penny of it."

At Bricker's side, the Scot burst into a single raucous peal of laughter. His muttonchop whiskers molded themselves for a moment into interesting new curves. He clapped the boy's shoulder. "Ye've got 'er pegged, lad. Ye've got 'er pegged." He wandered off wagging his head.

"The voyage may prove interesting after all. Have you had breakfast, boy?"

"Not yet, sir."

"Nor I." Bricker led off toward the galley. "You'll bring your things aboard soon as you've eaten and I'll tend to my business ashore. Are those your best clothes?"

"Uh, my only clothes, sir. We're not wealthy."

"You know the Wang See chandlery near here?"

"I've passed it, sir."

"Stop by there and have Wang See outfit you properly, including oilskins. We'll be crossing the south forties in summer, but it'll be cold all the same. I'll leave word it's to be put on *Arachne*'s tab."

"Thank-you, sir! Thank-you very much!"

"Don't thank me too profusely. It'll come out of your wages. Here we are." He ducked into the galley.

The Chinese cook peered into a big iron vat, frowning morosely. He shot the captain a perfunctory nod, all that was left of the elaborate bow with which he used to greet his employer. "Potatoes," he grumbled. "Cook, outside; inside, hard. Cook, inside; outside, apart pieces. Bah! Rice better." He looked at Eric and panic washed across his leathery face. "Gideon! Gone?"

"Very sick, but getting well. He'll stay here in Singapore until we can come back or send for him. Eric here is our cabin boy until Gideon returns. Eric, this is Wun Lin. Wun Lin, would you serve us both breakfast, please."

CHAPTER 2

Singapore, Midday, June 8, 1851

The morning flowed smoothly—delightfully smoothly, considering the way that Maude Harrington had started it off. Travis Bricker found the lady constantly on his mind as he wound through the stall-lined streets. Was she a supreme irritant or was she simply supremely lovely? There was a certain vulnerability, a desperation, behind the haughtiness. Bricker guessed she was a much nicer person than that first meeting would suggest. What grave concern did her pose as Queen of the Whole World conceal? What was the source of her conspicuous wealth? There was one sure way a white woman could come into a fortune quickly in Singapore, and Maude's superb face and figure would lend themselves to that means. Bricker realized belatedly where his thoughts were wandering. Mentally he apologized to the lady for thinking such evil thoughts about her, no doubt false besides.

He called upon the chandler, Wang See. The gentleman needed no clerks or warehouse boys, but the clerk of his friend Chow Chen had just married and moved to Kowloon.

Bricker called upon the chandler Chow Chen. Mr. Chow could indeed use a smart, quick boy. Could Gideon cipher? Affirmative. Could he read? Well, somewhat. The bargain was struck even before Bricker's tea had cooled enough to drink.

Gideon himself presented something of a different problem. Fever had left the boy less than alert. Bricker had a terrible time convincing him he was not being summarily abandoned. He explained to Gideon about the arrangement with Mr. Chow. He discussed the value to anyone planning to become a sea captain someday of a knowledge of chandlery. Once Gideon understood how ships' suppliers did business, he would know how to avoid being cheated or taken advantage of. That in itself would be worth the few months' separation.

Bricker promised to post a letter each time he called at a port. Several times over he solemnly pledged to return for Gideon—or send for him—as soon as health and trade permitted. Gideon would still have a berth aboard *Arachne* for as long as he chose. In saying goodby, Bricker held the boy close, firmly, for some minutes longer than really necessary.

He walked the long way around to the docks. Did that tiny streetside stall still operate on the Street of Bright Stars? It did. Did the wizened old lady there still sell those delectable bits of sweet curried duck? She did. The morning was absolutely faultless.

A block from Wang See's, the captain's brand-new cabin boy came popping out of nowhere, arms laden with parcels. Bricker was impressed all over again by the boy's quickness and charm.

The lad greeted him, jogged three paces ahead, and struck the exaggerated pose of a dandy gentleman. "Am I better attired now, sir?"

"Much better. Now don't outgrow everything before we raise England."

"I'll try not, sir." The boy marched along at his side a few moments. "Sir? You told Miss Harrington we'd be about a year getting to the North Atlantic."

"That's assuming no problems. I failed to mention to her that we were dismasted off the Society Islands not long ago, though we think we have the problem licked. But we haven't yet tried *Arachne* under a heavy press of sail. The Horn in December is usually as quiet as it ever gets, but it can always give you trouble, even on the west-east passage. We may call at Praia or Dakar, which would add a few weeks. London in June, Lord willing, as the roses begin to bloom."

"A long time, sir."

"A long way."

"Aye, a long way." The boy's voice faded, thoughtful. His eyes seemed misty. Was he saddened to leave the Far East or fearful of a new life alone in a different world? Bricker ought to get the lad talking.

"So you're going home to school. How much schooling have you had so far?"

"Not much, sir. A bit of Latin, but no Greek yet. And no geography. I could use some geography just now, to know where I am and where you're talking about."

"I'll try to remember that and be more informative."

The boy looked at him curiously. "Thank-you, sir. When you first said *'Arachne'* I thought you were saying *'Rackney'*. After all, ships have been given stranger names than that. But then I saw your quarterboards. Arachne was a Greek goddess, wasn't she?"

"No, a mortal. She considered herself the finest tapestry weaver in the world. This didn't sit well with Minerva, who was the goddess of such things. Arachne ended up challenging Minerva to a contest of tapestry-weaving skill. So Minerva stitched a big picture, telling how she gained control of Athens and had it named for her—her Greek name was Athena. And Arachne's tapestry pictured the gods' flaws and errors. Their shortcomings.''

"Wasn't very tactful, I daresay.''

"Wasn't tactful to challenge a goddess in the first place.''

"Who won?''

"Nobody. Minerva got fed up with her before they finished and turned her into a spider.''

"Why a—Oh! I see. That's why spiders are such incomparable weavers. So why did the owners name your boat *Arachne?*''

"Bark, not boat. Masts and tonnage of a ship but the mizzen fore-and-aft rigged.''

"I must learn all that?''

"It'll come. The owners had no prior contact with shipping. They came by her more or less by accident. Her rigging named her—that tangle of strange lines aloft. To them, her rigging was a web only Arachne could figure out.''

"Or Minerva.''

Bricker chuckled. "Or Minerva.'' He turned onto the street which led downhill to the wharfs. Food beckoned. The curried duck hadn't lasted long down there.

"I've so much to learn—ships and boats and barks, not to mention Minerva, who is Athens; no, Athena. And all that mythology. Sometimes I think—look! Isn't that Miss Harrington?'' The boy stretched out a burdened arm to point.

"It is!'' Bricker broke into a run without thinking.

Three-hundred yards ahead, Maude stood, flanked by two men. She shook her head violently. Her shrill protests were audible, even at this distance. Each man seized a blue-clad

21

elbow, and, as one, the three disappeared up a side street.

Bricker turned the corner so fast he nearly slipped in the mud. Billows of blue silk jounced along up ahead.

All three heard him coming. Miss Harrington twisted around. "Captain! Help me! Oh, help me!" She began struggling wildly, jerking, pulling, kicking. The elegant lady turned into quite a tornado.

Bricker didn't slow his pace. He aimed himself squarely at the taller of the two, then lunged aside suddenly to bowl the shorter over. He noted as an afterthought that the men were European, not Oriental.

Miss Harrington twisted free and, scooping up her skirts, ran down the street toward the docks. Bricker swung at Taller and missed completely. The man lunged at him, both fists flailing. Now Shorter was on his feet. With a soprano howl, Eric came flying through the air, parcels and all, and latched onto Shorter. The momentum carried the man down into the mud again.

Bricker slammed both fists into Taller's middle, struck again, and swung at the fellow's face. He connected this time, though not solidly enough. Taller tried to duck away, but was too slow. Bricker lined up a totally effective punch that slammed the man backwards into a jug-seller's stall.

Without pausing, Bricker wheeled to meet Shorter. Eric sat in the mud amongst his parcels, a splash of bright red on his mouth. Shorter was scrambling to his feet. A rolling water jug waddled into the edge of Bricker's vision. He snatched it up and flung it; he was quite as surprised as Shorter that his aim was true. The jug caught Shorter in the neck, giving Bricker time enough to reach the fellow with two good slugs. Shorter fell backward, his third roll in the mud.

Bricker grabbed two handfuls of shirt and hauled Eric to his feet. "Run, lad!"

Eric stared blankly at him, then snapped to life. He twisted around and scrambled in the mud, snatching up his parcels.

"I said run!"

"My things—"

In desperation Bricker grabbed the last bundle and shoved Eric in the right direction. The boy staggered before getting his feet moving. As soon as he was running strongly, Bricker gripped his arm and pulled him along. They were lucky for the moment; they must not push their luck or the Lord's good providence.

Bricker heard footsteps splacking in the mud behind them, but they were within sight of *Arachne* now. Bricker yelled. Up on the foredeck Halloran turned to look. They were safe now. Halloran came racing down the gangway as DuPres, aloft, jigged rapidly down the ratlines. The footbeats behind them ceased.

Bricker slowed to a walk. His lungs burned in the muggy air; sweat ran in rivers down his face. He let go of Eric's arm. The boy's knees buckled instantly. He sat in the mud a moment, swaying slightly, then stood. He slogged to the ship glassy-eyed, so winded he could not speak. The lad's face glowed alarmingly red. They both stumbled up the gangway with DuPres and Halloran right behind. Home.

"Halloran—Miss Harrington—Did she—?" Bricker sagged against the rail, unable to breathe either.

"Aye sir, She came running from upstreet there just a few minutes ago. Collapsed near the gangway into the loveliest pile of blue. Fisher's carried 'er aboard, but I've not been aft to know how she's doing."

"She didn't tell you to come help me?"

"Dead faint, sir. Never saw skin so white. A proper lady, I'd say, sir."

"Proper!" Bricker snorted. "Her trunks aboard yet?"

"Aye, all five of them. And the bags."

"Five?"

"Stowed 'em in the orlop, sir, except the two carpetbags. Opined she'd like them with her and stowed 'em in her quarters."

"Well done, Halloran. Tell McGovern and let's away. Send word when we're out in channel."

"Aye, sir!" Halloran jogged off foreward.

Bricker looked at his new cabin boy. The lad's face was still burning bright as a port light, but he could breathe somewhat. The blood on his lip and chin was turning black.

"You acquitted yourself well in that fight, lad. Waded right in. But when I give an order—any order—you're to obey instantly. Not when you get around to it, but instantly. Understand? As, for example, when I say, 'Run, lad!'"

"I'm sorry, sir." The lad gulped air. "Truly sorry." Those huge blue eyes drifted upward, totally repentant, to meet Bricker's. "I lost my head, sir." He took in another pound or two of air. "You said—all I could think of was—you said 'twas from my wages, sir."

CHAPTER 3

Entering Karimata Strait, Midday, June 10, 1851

The jib boom's tenor complaints betrayed its bobstays' need for retarring. The wind whistled under its soprano breath as it wove itself among the jib sails. The anchor bumped, baritone, against its billboard in rhythm with the rise and fall of *Arachne*'s prow. The cutwater's alto swish was soft and sibilant.

Bricker stood in his favorite place at the foredeck railing and braced one foot against the cathead, listening to this gentle symphony of hums and whispers. He knew every sound his ship was capable of making—any captain knew that—and these sounds pleased him most. They were the contented voices of a vessel doing what she did best, clipping along before a stiff breeze off her starboard quarter. *Arachne* was not often blessed with such a fair breeze, even less often on a day as sunny and clear as this. Bricker basked in the pure pleasure of the moment.

"Excuse me, sir. I completed all the tasks you mentioned. What shall I do next?"

Bricker turned to his cabin boy. "The serving closet is

cleared away? The cabin tidied? The lamp chimneys polished?''

"Aye, sir. I trimmed the wick in the lamp above the table. It was burning a bit smoky this morning.''

"Mmm.'' Bricker settled back against the rail with both elbows. "Excellent, young Eric. Well, then, you're free to move about as you like till tea time.''

" 'As I like'?'' Eric cleared his throat. "Ah, sir? Would I be disturbing you if I stay right here?''

"Not at all. Welcome.''

Eric flashed that quick and cheerful grin. "Thank-you, sir!'' He leaned against the rail in partial imitation of his captain, though the position jacked his elbows up shoulder high. He presently stretched to tiptow to peer over the side, watching their cutwater.

Such a simple thing, a boy watching a cutwater, but it instantly took Bricker back twenty-five years. He had been too short to reach the toprail then, and thus spent hours stretched out precariously across the jib. Most curious of all, that boyhood fondness persisted. He could still watch, fascinated, for hours on end.

Eric waved a finger toward the water. "I've heard it said, sir, that it glows at night.'' The eyes flicked up at him. "Is it true?''

"Yes. Sometimes in certain seasons and in certain waters. Phosphorescence. A gentle green or blue, very pale. Muted. But on a dark night it looks almost vivid. The color boils up and then fades as it moves out and away from the vessel.''

"I'd love to see that sometime.''

"I'll tell the watches to call you if they notice it.''

"Would you really?'' Eric stared at him a moment, apparently realized it was impolite, and turned his eyes back to the roiling water. "When will we lose sight of land?''

"Not for a while. These particular waters are riddled with little islands; almost always a few visible through the strait here."

"We're passing between Sumatra and Borneo, right?"

"Right. Sumatra lies west of the Java Sea, and Celebes lies east. We're paralleling the Indonesian Islands—Batavia's just about due south of us—but you won't see them. Too far away."

"I should think we'd see more ships, though, for all the tea and spices they send to the world."

Bricker smiled at the simplicity of his logic. "Just local traffic through here. Major trade routes follow the prevailing winds north from Singapore through the China Sea."

"China Sea. Pirates."

"Used to be. The pirates are pretty well suppressed. The Portuguese cleaned up the area around Macao, the British cleaned up around Sarawak and Borneo."

"So there aren't any anymore?"

"Oh, there are *some*. But it's not at all like it was."

"Then that's why you just stand here and look contented. I was afraid to ask, but now I know. You're relieved that there aren't any pirates to chase us."

Bricker laughed. "I've been chased by pirates, and recently. No, I'm just standing here feeling good because I gambled and won for once."

"You don't appear to be a gambling man."

"I mentioned the prevailing winds take ships north into the China Sea. I could have looped the long way around to my destination by following the normal wind patterns. I took a chance and headed straight east instead; much shorter, but that doesn't necessarily mean faster." He waved a hand. "The breeze is perfect; totally opposite to the way it usually blows at this time of year. Better than I could have hoped for.

27

"I see. Then you're standing here, gloating."

"And listening to the music."

The boy frowned, caught off guard. "Really! Music?"

"I attended a concert in London a few years ago. A Handel oratorio. The woman I escorted was enthralled by the way all the singers sang different things, essentially, yet it all fit together. One whole. I didn't say this to her, but I hear that every day. *Arachne* has her special set of voices. They change—for example, during heavy weather—but she always harmonizes with herself and with the Nereids' songs." Bricker glanced at his cabin boy. The frown had deepened. He smiled to himself. "Listen to the swish of water along the hull here. Hear the rhythm? And a melody of sorts. Nereids singing."

Eric strained at tiptoe. He dropped down on his heels and studied Bricker. "Little things singing down there? What are Nee-ree-ids?"

"More classical mythology. Learn the classics well. Much of literature refers to it; the planets and constellations all reflect it; even scientific names of many plants and animals come from it. Do you know what a nymph is?"

"A pretty maiden. A demigoddess."

"That's right. Nereids were sea nymphs, daughters of the gods Nereus and Doris."

"In the *Odyssey,* wasn't Calypso a sea nymph?"

"Very good. She was."

"I thought Neptune was god of the sea, not Nereus."

"Oceanus was, until the old Titans were overthrown and Neptune took the job. Nereus was Neptune's father-in-law. An aquatic elder statesman, you might say—a wise and well-spoken thinker. I'd like to think that at least some of his fifty daughters inherited that wisdom. That they know a sound vessel when she plies their waters and that they enjoy singing in concert with her."

28

Those splendid eyes were saucers. "You actually believe that?"

"No, I said I would like to think that. What I actually believe is that the one true God is Lord of the sea, as He is Lord of everything else in earth and heaven. In Jeremiah 31—somewhere around verse 30 or 35, I think—the prophet says the Lord stirs up the sea so the waves roar. And in Matthew 8, of course, Jesus stilled the storm at sea. And then there's Jonah."

A cool distance seemed to wash across Eric momentarily. Then he warmed again. "Nereids' singing. I wish you taught mythology in a school. Minerva, Arachne, Nereus—I'd study there. You make them seem alive."

"Why, thank-you." Bricker pondered what, exactly, the charm of this boy might be. He admired his captain quite obviously and that always endeared one. His intelligence and sense of wonder, his industry were all most appealing. Bricker admired those traits in any person, but that did not seem quite it. And the boy was physically attractive to the eye—slim, slight, pleasant features, even say pretty features. He'd never be a big man, but he'd be a lady-killer.

A dark cloud cooled Bricker's thoughts. He had never encountered the instance firsthand, but he had heard enough whispered stories—shipmasters who found a boy attractive and employed him for immoral purposes. Surely that wasn't possible here. Bricker would never even consider such a heinous sin. Yet the blackest of perversions must start somewhere, and perhaps, in just such innocent thought. No. No, the more he thought about it, the further Bricker put that sort of thing out of his mind. This boy, not nearly a man yet, was simply pleasant company.

His close attention bolstered Bricker's self-esteem; Eric listened. And his sensitivity made conversation a pleasure. Bricker did more than just put any impure thoughts out of his mind. He banished any further consideration of them. As time permitted he would enjoy the lad's innocent company. Then he would set the boy ashore in London and sign some other cabin boy for the voyage out, assuming Gideon was not with them.

Eric laid his chin on his arms. "When I complete my duties, as now, do I really have time all to my own, to do as I please?"

Bricker reminded himself that this boy, however delightful, was still a boy, and a clever one at that. "Within limits. So long as what you please isn't bound to get you into trouble if it's discovered. I know boys will be boys, but not aboard my vessel. I hope you've left any pranks ashore in Singapore."

Eric giggled. "I'd never pull pranks on you, sir. That Maude Harrington, perhaps—she deserves some trouble—but not you. Nor shall I bother her. I'll behave."

"You sound jealous, boy."

"Jealous! What have I in common with her?"

"Nothing, I would presume. That's why your general tone of voice puzzles me."

"I suppose it's her attitude, sir, as if we were all born to serve her highness. If I were a lady, sir, and not what I am—that is, if I were vying for your attention—I've heard that women may fight over a man that way—I'd say to her—" Eric drew himself up stiffly. "I'd say to her, 'Miss Harrington, you may have him!' Forgive my boldness, sir."

Bricker tried to hide his grin and almost succeeded. "And what fault do you find in me that I'm not worth fighting over?"

"None, sir. These crewmen all put out their very best for you and seem to enjoy doing it. That says what sort of master you are, though I've no experience as a seaman myself. I mean, I can't speak to that firsthand. There is, though—ah, I'm not certain I should say this—"

"I promise I won't remember it, let alone repeat it."

"Then, sir, my only objection is not a fault. It's, ah, that you tend to dwell on religious things. I've had religion pumped down me my whole life—my parents and my brother-in-law, all telling me God will punish me if I don't behave. They painted the picture of a huge ship with God as the Master, applying His cat-o'-nine-tails liberally to all His erring little crewmen. Frankly, sir, I've been rather confused about religion of late, and I'd like not to even think about it for a while. 'Twould be a pleasant change from what my life has been so far."

"I see. So you'd be happiest if I put God aside completely. Then you'd have no objections to me at all."

"I'm sorry, sir, but yes."

"Then I won't preach to you or require your attendance at the services we hold each Sunday. But I can't put my God aside any more than I can leave my left leg behind. He's part of me. However, I understand that you must work out—"

"Sail ho!" the lookout's voice interrupted from on high.

Bricker twisted around and called up into the straining canvas, "Where away?"

"Dead astern."

Bricker pushed away from the rail and walked briskly aft. Eric was running to keep up.

"Your duty, lad, is always to fetch my telescope when the lookout calls. I'll expect it without asking. It's on my desk."

"Aye, sir!" The boy ducked aside and in the cabin door as Bricker took the quarterdeck steps two at a time. He leaned on the taffrail to watch the white fleck on the horizon.

McGovern's square frame came to rest beside him. "In a

31

hurry, she is; evensay pursuing us. Pirates, mayhap.''

"Or simply an English vessel wishing to send mail east.''

Eric bounded to the rail and handed him his telescope. Bricker snapped it open and tried to pick out her colors, but she was still too distant. He heard the patter of light slippers behind him as he handed the glass off to McGovern.

Maude Harrington, her skirts flowing in the breeze, paused by his elbow. "You can outrun them, can't you, Captain?''

"Unless they be pirates, why should I?''

"You must!'' Her eyes opened wide, fear-filled. The long lashes framed them in black, making their rich brown richer. "Please, Captain!''

"Miss Harrington, the men who accosted you just before we sailed were hardly waterfront ruffians out to earn a pound or two from a kidnapping. They were Europeans, fairly well dressed, and had seen a barber recently. I believe someone employed them, which means you're running away from someone or something.''

"Captain, you'd best not be intimating that I'm a fugitive from the law or anything of that sort.''

"I see her colors. British.'' McGovern squinted into the glass. "Arrgh! They just touched one off!''

Bricker saw the tiny puff of blue. The water splashed between his ship and theirs; belatedly, a muffled little boom floated in off their wake.

McGovern scowled. "Shall we come up?''

"No. Put on some canvas and let's see how we do. I don't trust her colors when she acts that uncivil.''

"Aye!'' The Scotsman almost smiled as he hurried off. Nearly as much as Bricker, the first mate loved a good run.

"I'm not familiar with the jargon.'' Miss Harrington watched the fleck, transfixed. "Does this mean we're running away?''

"For the time, at least. Pirates have been known to fly the Union Jack or some other friendly colors. Then, you see, they come roaring down unsuspected on their prey. But that vessel carries twice the sail area we do. I doubt we can outpace them for long."

Her soft lips trembled. "I see. Please do your best, Captain."

Bricker studied the lovely face, the milky skin. Those soft lips tightened into a thin, hard line. Her fingers diddled nervously. Sometime, under the right circumstance, Bricker would draw out of her the reason for this extreme agitation. For now he contented himself with feeling sorry for her. She was sorely perplexed. For all her aloofness, her coldness, she was so vulnerable. It touched him. He glanced at Eric. It wasn't touching his cabin boy at all. The lad watched her furtively, not the least bit sympathetic.

The royals snapped, luffed momentarily and spread to the breeze. McGovern was ordering Edward and one other to wing the spencer out wide. Never could Bricker ignore this lady—this vessel—when she was flying. When the breeze was right and *Arachne* was stretched out full like this she lost her status as an inanimate object. Some people claimed that the best captains always fell in love with their ships. In a peculiar sense it was quite true.

How long had he stood there absorbing the pleasure of her running? He snapped his attention back to the problem at hand—or was it a problem? He looked behind. Their pursuer was drawing closer by the minute.

CHAPTER 4

Off Cape Sambar, Teatime, June 10, 1851

Adrenalin flowing with the thrill of the chase, Bricker took the quarterdeck steps two at a time. Just as he reached the taffrail their pursuer fired another warning shot. Fisher came springing up the steps with his normal ebullience, and Eric bounded along right behind him.

Fisher greeted the helmsman in passing and draped himself across the rail. "Me insignificant opinion be that we'll not outrun 'er. And it's too early in the day to 'ope we can keep a'ead till dark and steal away."

"I agree. Miss Harrington is staying out of sight?"

"By 'er own request. She's absolutely certain that vessel's coming to lop off 'er dear sweet 'ead."

"The cabin is not sufficient. Hide her thoroughly and completely in whatever way your nimble mind contrives. Hide her well. If the vessel's legitimate and they've come seeking her, they won't get her unless they show good reason to have her. And if they're pirates, it's absolutely imperative she not be found."

Fisher glowed. "I consider it a privilege to render the lady temporarily invisible."

"And, Fisher. Tell Halloran to break out the guns and arm the crew—everyone save Eric here."

"On me way!" Fisher romped off across the quarterdeck and descended toward the cabin without touching the steps at all.

"Sir?" Eric's voice quavered a bit. "You really think they're pirates? That they might do something—ah—awful?"

"It's possible, but not probable. I told you piracy is dying out."

"On the main shipping lanes, you said. We failed to discuss the Java Sea."

Bricker smiled. "This is a major route west part of the year. Don't fret until fretting is necessary. Besides, they might kill the men and ravish the women, but they usually don't harm boys."

"Scant comfort that is."

Bricker raised his glass. "There's a crewman. Two. Both dressed like proper British seamen."

"But if they be pirates, do I fight, too?"

"No." He lowered his glass. "No, Eric. You did bravely with those two in Singapore, but compared to your average pirate they were inept. Sorry fighters. You'd be no match for a real cutthroat. So keep out of the way. Should shooting start, we don't want to worry about whether you might be in the line of fire. Understand?"

"Yes, sir," the boy barely whispered. Bricker looked at Eric's eyes. Intriguing. Brown is supposed to be warm and puppy-dog, yet Maude Harrington's eyes were cold. Blue is considered aloof and haughty, but young Eric's blue eyes were warm and soft. Obviously it was not color after all, so much as what lay behind the eyes.

"Sir?" Halloran came up behind and handed him his pistol. "And your two extra cylinders. Fisher put DuPres up in the rigging with the shotgun. And we have our instructions to forget there's a lady aboard.''

"Then spill our canvas and bring her about. Eric, make yourself scarce.'' Bricker slipped the ungainly pistol into his pocket. He let his hand linger a moment on the smooth, cool grip. "Death at y'r fingertips'' McGovern called it. McGovern detested guns of any kind, though this very pistol had once saved the first mate's life.

Their pursuer ranged alongside. No wonder she overhauled them so quickly. She had enough canvas aloft to shade a small city. Every man aboard her appeared to be a proper seaman and she was fitted as a proper merchantman. Her quarterboards said *Joseph Whidby*.

Fisher handed Bricker his bullhorn as he stepped up to the port railing, but he didn't need it. The merchantman wallowed less than fifty feet to port. At the rail beside her captain, a short, stocky Malay in some sort of paramilitary uniform called out, "Prepare to receive boarders!" Already four seamen were lowering a jolly boat.

Fisher snorted derisively. "Friendly jack, aye? The sort of man whose wassail y'd love to sip on Christmas Eve.''

"He has six armed men coming over with him. Do you recognize the uniforms?''

"Nay, unless they be Singapore civilian militia. Constables. That'd be the governor's boys.''

"The guns look like muskets. Your guess sounds good.'' Bricker shouted, "What does Singapore's governor want with us?''

"We've come for Maude Harrington.''

"Begorra!" Fisher mumbled under his breath. "Ye pegged that one right on the beacon!''

"She's well hidden?''

"Aye. And cleverly, if I do say so meself.''

Bricker watched the jolly boat bob toward them and recalled the desperation and fear in Maude Harrington's troubled eyes. Fisher and Halloran dropped a ladder over the side. In a rush the seven militiamen—or whatever they were—swarmed up onto the deck.

Their leader snapped a brusque salute. "Maude Harrington, Captain. A reliable informant assured us she's aboard."

"So Maude Harrington is a mortal woman. You must have a dandy reason to come storming after her like this commandeering a merchantman. Must be an intriguing story."

"We know she's here. Give her over to us now, or you can return to Singapore in irons and give her to us there."

Bricker felt his neck getting warm. "I doubt whatever authority you enjoyed in Singapore extends onto the high seas. You're proposing piracy, and we take a dim view of piracy. If you think you can pit six muskets against my armed crew, why, then I suppose you'll try to put me in irons. Bet you're smarter'n that."

"My authority is vested by the governor and, therefore, the crown." The Malay dropped his voice to a condescending purr. "I didn't commandeer the *Whidby* to pass the time of day with you. I do indeed have full authority to recover Miss Harrington by whatever means I must. You're not beyond jurisdiction of the Straits Settlements. You'll be wise to surrender her with no further fuss."

Bricker stepped back, in part to avoid the man's breath. "Mr. Fisher, Mr. McGovern; these gentlemen have permission to make a hasty search of our vessel. Follow them about, let them satisfy themselves as to the presence or absence of any Maude Harrington."

The commander eyed Bricker suspiciously. Suddenly he snapped something in Tamil. The six musketeers marched aft. Four of them disappeared into the stern cabin. The other

37

two bounded up the quarterdeck steps. At a loss for anything impressive to do, the commander stationed himself halfway between Bricker and the aft companionway.

"Ohmigawsh!" Fisher snarled under his breath. "I forgot about 'er ditty! She must 'ave foofoo things scattered all over 'er quarters. They'll know for sure there's a lady aboard, and any moment now!"

Bricker seethed. He wanted dearly to explode on the outside, of course, but he dared not. He hissed, "I left that to you, Bosun, and hiding her possessions was surely a part of hiding *her*."

The Malay was frowning toward them, trying to eavesdrop.

Bricker raised his voice a notch. "The next time we run out of my favorite coffee two days into a voyage, Bosun, you'll be deposited ashore at the nearest port of call. Is that understood?"

Fisher kowtowed so sincerely he actually tugged his forelock. "Ah, Cap'n, I cannae tell ye 'ow truly sorry I am! And I assure ye 'twill not 'appen again!"

The four came marching out the stern cabin with McGovern at their heels. They frowned at their commander with a negative little shake of the head and tromped down the aft companionway. McGovern and the other two followed. The commander snooped along the main deck, sticking his nose in here and lifting that.

Bricker studied Fisher and Fisher stared back. "Go tend your duties, Bosun. And our seven guests will not be staying for dinner. Let them eat aboard their commandeered vessel."

"I shall thus inform the chef, sir."

Chef. Wun lin a chef. Much as Bricker wanted to be enraged at his bosun he found himself smiling—almost. He casually wandered aft and pushed through the cabin door.

Eric was setting the table for tea. The guest cabin door stood open. The bed there was neatly made up and tucked in, the room devoid of any personal belongings whatever. Bricker yanked open a locker under the bed. Empty. The room had not been used for a long time. To the searching eye, Maude Harrington had never existed.

Presently Bricker wandered back out on deck. He ordered the main staysail set to keep *Arachne* a safer distance off *Whidby*'s beam. He delivered some course corrections to the helm and rapped his knuckles on the water butt. Full.

Finally, after half an eternity, the Malay gave up. In a very black mood indeed, he scowled up at Bricker as his jolly boat bobbed away, his six musketeers straining at the oars. They rowed like lubbers.

"Shall I wave bye-bye, Capt'n?" Fisher hauled the rope ladder in.

"I think not. You'd undoubtedly wave with your thumb to your nose, and that's not polite."

Fisher slammed the rail into place. "Ye've the general idea right enough. Cheeky fellow. Pity 'e'll never know 'e was right all along."

The jolly boat thunked against the flanks of *Joseph Whidby*. The oarsmen staved her off as the Malay hauled himself awkwardly up their ladder. The *Whidby*'s captain waved to Bricker, a hearty glad-it's-over saluting gesture.

Bricker waved back just as heartily. "Mr. McGovern, set our sails and get us underway again. Mr. Fisher, you may resurrect our passenger. Be prepared to tuck her away again, though, should they come about."

"Me pleasure, sir." Fisher cavorted off.

Bricker walked back to the stern cabin. It was well past teatime, but all their meals would be late tonight. Wun Lin had had to tear his galley apart for that constable—or whatever he was.

Eric set a steaming teapot on the table. "Your tea is ready, sir. Will the bosun and first mate be coming?"

"Mr. McGovern'll be late; save him some. Mr. Fisher will be here shortly with Miss Harrington. Eric, are you responsible for hiding her belongings?"

The boy smiled in guarded pride. "I wasn't sure I should, at first. But when no one else came to do it, I thought I'd better. Did I act out of line?"

"You did splendidly. Fisher thought of it too late. But where did you put all that stuff?"

Eric swung his closet door open. "The carpetbags are in my locker here. I jammed my oilskins into the tops of them to make them appear my own. Her soap and face paints are wrapped in her towels. I hid them among the other towels in the serving closet here. And her shoes are folded in amongst the shirts in your locker, sir, and her hair brushes are—" Eric's brow furrowed. "Now where did I put them? Ah, well, sir. They're about here somewhere."

Bricker laughed. He could see the *Whidby* departing, already far astern. The tension was gone, the situation relieved. They could enjoy the remainder of the voyage as it had gone thus far—pleasant and peaceful. There was no reason to suspect exceptionally foul weather this time of year. He would quiz Miss Harrington closely about this turn of events. Perhaps he would teach young Eric chess, or ask Wun Lin to teach him backgammon, or both.

Eric was glowing. "Rather exciting, wasn't it—I mean the suspense. Wondering if they might find her. Do you know where Fisher hid her, sir?"

Bricker heard muffled voices approaching. "No, but I'm sure we'll find out. Fisher's much too proud of his little *coup* to keep it to himself." He poured three cups of tea. Eric popped a tea cozy over the pot; his fingers were deft, quick, and very clean, unusual for a lad that age.

The cabin door burst open. Maude Harrington filled the cabin instantly with her strident shouting. "—so humiliated! Never! Nor shall I ever be again, you dimwitted Irishman!" She fixed her blazing eyes on Bricker. "And you—you ordered it! You condoned it! How could you?!"

Bricker stood, partly in politeness, mostly in surprise. "I don't understand your consternation, Miss Harrington." He glanced at Fisher but the answer wasn't there. Fisher shrugged in blank confusion.

"You don't understand?! *Look at me!* My dress is spoilt! Ruined! I'll never get this filth out of my hair! I reek! In a slop barrel, that's where he dumped me! A slop barrel! He poured slop on top of me and nailed the lid shut. I had to breathe through a knothole in the stave for two hours.

Fisher grimaced. "And lucky we are the barrel 'ad a knothole. We wouldn't 'ave been able to nail the lid down for fear of suffocating 'er. As it was, we—"

"'*Lucky*'!" She shrieked. She turned on Fisher. Her string of expletives included two Bricker had never heard in twenty-five years at sea. She stomped off to her quarters, shedding potato parings.

Bricker pointed to the floor. "Eric, clean up that garbage before someone slips or ma—"

"They're gone!" She came howling out of her cabin and stopped at the table, the picture of perfect rage. "Everything's gone!"

"Of course! I'd forgotten. Mr. Fisher, would you dig her shoes out of my shirt locker, please? Eric, fetch her carpetbags and towels from the closet. And try to remember what you did with her hairbrushes."

She pointed wildly at Eric. "You mean this hideous boy has been pawing through my private belongings? You permitted this half-sized waif to rummage through my personal things? How could—"

41

"You—you ingrate!" Eric exploded so violently that Bricker was momentarily dumbstruck. "The slop barrel's better by far than you deserve! If it weren't for the captain and Bosun Fisher you'd be on your way to Singapore in the clutches of a greasy little martinet, and good riddance! They risked much for you. They—"

"That's enough!" Bricker bellowed.

Even as he spoke, Maude had seized the teapot. She hurled it at Eric with perfect aim; it thunked against his chest, splashed steaming tea all down the front of him. He yelped soprano in pain and surprise.

Bricker waved toward the serving closet. "Go dash cold water on it, lad! Quickly!"

Eric wheeled and fled, slamming the closet door behind him.

Bricker did not bother to walk around the table. In one stride he was atop it; one more took him to stand on the floor in front of this deranged lady. "The boy spoke out of turn, but he's absolutely right. Your ingratitude is distressing and out of place. Not only could we have been saved considerable inconvenience by turning you over to them, we were no doubt outside the law in hiding you. And we did it knowing nothing about you. You probably deserve to be sent back. We could all be in irons right now, had they found you. And here you have the impertinence to scream at us for taking considerable risk on your behalf. For hiding you well enough that they scoured this vessel without finding you. You owe us a great deal more than the price of passage, madam, and if you can't repay with graciousness, you will at least repay with silence."

He clamped onto her arm and dragged her off to her cabin. He gave her a push through the door, not too gently, and slammed it after her. He called through the panel. "We'll put your belongings in as we come across them,

Miss Harrington. Consider yourself confined to quarters."

He took a deep breath, then another, for the first one failed utterly to control his ire. Fisher emerged from his quarters with an armload of shoes, chewing his lip.

"I compliment you, Mr. Fisher. You did well both in hiding her successfully and in keeping a civil tongue. You're an officer and a gentleman."

"Ah, well, thankee, sir. I knew I was an officer." Fisher raised a hand to rap on the lady's door, hesitated and turned. "I 'ope, sir, ye'll not consider y'r own reaction a breach of chivalry. 'Twas the perfect response for the occasion, sir. Couldn't 've said it better meself. And 'ere they claim we Irish 'as the gift of blarney!"

Bricker chuckled. "Thank-you, Bosun. Carry on." As he headed for the serving closet, he thought he heard Fisher mumble, "Wouldn't I love to" but he wasn't certain, nor was he about to ask. He stepped into the serving closet and closed the door behind him, lest the irate Miss Harrington storm back out and accidentally see young Eric in a state of undress.

Bricker froze . . . He stared . . . His mind went blank.

Eric . . . was . . . Erica!

CHAPTER 5

Entering the Java Sea, Past teatime, June 10, 1851

Bricker knew some deepwater captains were famous for their flamboyance, their love of risk and high adventure. He was not one of them. He enjoyed routine, at least to a point. He approached life deliberately, evensay cautiously at times. And he vastly preferred the predictable. Surprises tended to incapacitate him, and he had just been struck by two surprises in a row.

The erstwhile cabin boy stood before him utterly naked. She flung one arm across her breasts and with the other hand covered her most private parts. The gesture was futile. Her breasts, the curve of her waistline and hips was enough to tell him her true sex.

After what seemed a century or two of being unable to think or move, Bricker wheeled and presented his back to her. All he could think to ask was, "Why?"

Apparently surprises paralyzed her also. "I had no other— I didn't— you don't understand. There was no other way— I—" Oilskins rustled; the stool creaked. Her voice had been reined in to some sort of control. "I am robed now, sir."

He turned cautiously. She sat perched on the high stool beside the counter. Her top was completely covered by her oilskin jacket, and her lower half was almost adequately swathed in towels. She stared at the floor. Tears streamed down her cheeks.

"You are the young woman who directed me to the doctor that night. The supposed sister."

She nodded and sniffled.

"I believe I deserve some explanation."

The huge blue eyes drifted up to meet his. "I'd rather not. Must I?"

"Yes, you must!" His voice exploded much too loudly. He cleared his throat and modulated his ranting. "At the very least you've betrayed my confidence. You've placed me in a difficult and compromising position. Should anyone else learn who you really are— I mean what you really are—"

"They won't." She was studying him almost in a calculating way, sizing him up. Did she realize to what a blithering idiot her little surprise had reduced him? It seemed she did. "I assure you, sir, they won't. I've been serving you well as a cabin boy, have I not?"

"Yes, you have. I can't fault you for that. But—"

"Then let it continue so." She raised a hand. "In the first place, I swear I'll throw myself overboard before I'll spend one minute with that witch in guest quarters. You've nowhere else to put me but here. So let me continue serving as I have been. You need a cabin boy and I do well to keep my identity a secret. What I'm trying to say, I suppose, is that you needn't make any hasty decisions right this moment. Nothing is lost by letting things go along as they have been."

"But you're not a— I mean you are a—" He stopped. She was right, for all her deceit. He could do nothing at this moment, but not because he wanted things to continue. He could think of nothing to do. His mind was blank. She sat, unmoving and quite composed, watching him, clutching that jacket around her.

"What's your true name?"

"Erica Rollin Rice. Margaret is my middle name."

"Where is your husband now?"

"Joshua Rice died about a year ago. I'm a widow."

"You're too young to be a widow."

"I'm twenty. I married at eighteen, which is not so very young."

Married at eighteen, nubile, still young and lovely, self-possessed—

Bricker turned away and studied the dishes on the shelf. The appearance and the thought of her were leading his mind astray. He'd best redirect his mind before his body got the notion to follow. "You haven't yet answered my first question. Why?"

"I saw in you my only chance to return home to England honorably."

"'Honorably.' A strange use of the word, Mrs. Rice. You lie and deceive in the basest way and call it honorable."

"I realize you think precious little of me just now."

"That is understatement."

"But you'd think even less of me if I poured out all the details of these last few years. Yes, Captain, I am honorable. Fortunately, my good honor springs not from what you think of me, but from what I am—and will be. Please don't press me further. Later perhaps. Sometime. But not now."

He was master of this vessel; his word was law. He could extract the truth from her by sheer dint of his authority. But would it be the truth? What, as Pilate asked Jesus, is truth?

46

He found himself saying more than he had intended, more than he ought. He turned to her. "I enjoyed talking to you very much. You make pleasant company. After dinner, as you readied the table and we were teasing each other, this morning on the foredeck—two days out and you were brightening the voyage already. I suppose that's why I feel so betrayed now. I'm sorry you are who you are. I liked Eric very much." He turned to leave but twisted around again. "I, uh, failed to notice. Your burns. Were you badly scalded?"

"No. No blisters. Just a bit of redness. I did as you said and splashed cold water on it. I suspect it will disappear in a day or so. Thank you for asking, sir."

He nodded. He had trouble saying that name now. "See to yourself, Eric. And check with Wun Lin about supper."

"Aye, sir." The voice whispered as if stricken. It sounded almost like the hushed swishing of the Nerieds.

Bricker closed the door behind him.

Fisher was down on his knees peering under Bricker's desk, his ear to the floor. He vaulted to his feet. "Sure'n I 'ope young Eric remembers the whereabouts of the lady's 'airbrushes, for meself cannae turn 'em up."

"She can live without them." Bricker was done with women of any stripe. *Bah*.

The volatile Irishman dissolved into instant worry. "The lad's badly burned, sir?"

"No. The burns are superficial. Be gone in a day or two."

The face rearranged itself to its customary grin. "Ah." He bounced across the cabin.

Bricker realized almost too late where his bosun was headed. He wheeled. "Mr. Fisher!"

Fisher paused with his hand on the serving closet door. "Aye, sir?"

"There's nothing you need in there."

Fisher frowned. "I thought ye mentioned the lady's bags are there."

"Eric can bring them out in good time."

The frown deepened. Fisher's shrug was a suspicious gesture rather than a resigned one.

Bricker groped for some reason, any reason— "The lad's undressed and he's still at that bashful age. Self-conscious. He'll be out when he's ready."

The face relaxed. "Of course, and well I remember. There was a while there, when meself was yet a shaver, I went through the same sort of thing." He strode toward the door. "Didn't want me own Mum to see me peeled. She put an end to that nonsense quick enough; claimed she changed me nappies long enough that me bottom 'eld no secrets for 'er." He disappeared outside.

The noise Fisher generated by his very presence left with him. The room was suddenly, instantly, dreadfully silent. Bricker took a quiet turn around the cabin. He heard dramatic sobbing from Maude Harrington's guest quarters and sniffling from the serving closet. He glanced out the casement window to the rear. *Whidby* had nearly disappeared. He flopped down in his chair. He tried to be God's man toward everyone in the whole world. Why was life so wickedly unfair in return? By slow degrees the silence cooled his jangled nerves and thoughts.

Fisher swooped back in the door with a new teapot from stores. The silence fled. Eric emerged, red-eyed, from the closet. He dropped a towel on the pool of tea and pushed it about with one foot.

Fisher handed him the pot. "Ask Wun Lin for a reload."

"Aye, sir." Eric left.

Fisher disappeared into the serving closet and returned moments later with the carpetbags.

"Eric says he put some of his own things in them to disguise them." Bricker reflected momentarily on the boy/girl's cleverness.

"Noticed, sir. Bright lad. I think I've removed everything not belonging to a lady."

That's what you think. Bricker watched him cross the room. Fisher knocked, announced his intentions and received some sort of muffled acknowledgment. He cracked the door open just far enough to scoot the bags inside and carefully, quietly closed it again.

Fisher turned. "Ye know, I'm sure, why every ship's a she. Moody. Unpredictable. Y'r source of pain and pleasure. Then about the time ye give y'r 'eart and soul over to 'er, she sinks right out from under ye and leaves ye to the bitter sharks of fate. Ah, but what would we ever do without 'em, eh?"

"You'll do without that one. She's very likely married, and I'll not countenance adultery aboard this vessel."

"O' course, sir. Furthest thing from me mind." He dropped to one knee and began mopping up tea. "Pitiful sight she is, too, all sprawled out upon 'er bunk so sad; one dainty ankle draped fetchingly over the end of it; the pale shoulders trembling as she sobs 'er little—"

"Belay that!"

"Aye, sir."

Eric returned with the tea and set it on the table. "Wun Lin promises dinner in two hours, sir."

"Thank-you."

A shaft of golden evening sun stabbed through the stern window and splashed across the floor.

Eric returned Maude's towel and toiletries to her. He/she seemed to share none of Fisher's awe and admiration for women. Now that Bricker reflected on it, Eric's attitude toward Miss Harrington was nowhere near what one would expect from a boy. Boys fear strange women, hold them in abeyance. Eric despised her as an equal. Bricker should have seen that right away. What had blinded him?

The golden shaft widened out to a dazzling sheet of light. It reflected into Bricker's eyes.

Fisher glanced at his captain. "Shall I be mother of the pot today, sir?"

"Go ahead." Bricker hauled himself to his feet and shuffled to the table, feeling old before his time. He sat down as Fisher poured all around.

Fisher patted the chair to his left. "Eric, me lad, sit down 'ere. With all the 'uggermugger swirling about, ye deserve to be treated like a person this once. 'Ave some tea with us."

"It's all right, sir, really . . ."

"Sit."

Eric sat.

Fisher pushed Miss Harrington's cup in front of Eric. "Ye see, lad, it occurs to me belatedly that the chief reason y'r chest was scalded so is simply that ye were defending y'r ship's officers—a noble gesture. 'Ad ye let injustice reign and kept y'r mouth shut, ye would never 'ave come to grief. So therefore the captain and meself, we owe ye a considerable debt of gratitude. Aye, Cap'n?"

"Gratitude," Bricker muttered.

"Mmm. Well. Anyway. The captain at times fails to articulate 'is true feelings, but I take that as an opportunity to thank ye on behalf of us both. Y're a true and loyal mate and I for one am tickled pink y're aboard." He looked pointedly at Bricker. "Aye, sir?"

"Uh—of course. Tickled pink." Bricker glared at Eric. Eric stared at the table.

Fisher rolled on undaunted. "And from all this, lad, y've

learned two important lessons today. One is that ye never speak 'arshly to an irate female or call attention to y'rself, regardless 'ow lovely 'er form and figure. Sure 'n she'll nail ye one way or t'other. And the second: When something unexpected pops up, rest assured y'r captain 'ere is competent to 'andle it; but it does put 'im off. So when 'e's been dealt an unexpected card, just back off awhile. 'E'll sweeten up soon enough.''

Fisher patted Eric's shoulder, his hand lingering a moment. *A man should never casually touch a woman, and even less so in such an intimate manner,* thought Bricker. Fisher wrapped his arm about Eric's shoulders and gave him a final avuncular hug. ''Y're a member of the crew, lad, and welcome ye are.''

''Thank-you, sir,'' Eric mumbled.

Bricker sipped his tea and burned his tongue. How long could this impossible charade go on before someone noticed that Eric was not what he pretended to be? The deception had been unmasked, at least to himself, in less than forty-eight hours. Would his crew believe he had signed Eric on unwittingly? Hardly. So far his best bet would be to protect Eric's secret as long as possible and listen for murmuring among his men. If the secret went undiscovered to that point he might deposit Eric at the nearest port of call without anyone being the wiser. Embarrassing, to have been taken in so easily by this deceit.

The cabin door banged open. McGovern crossed to the table and stopped. He looked from face to face, scowling. ''What's wrong?''

Bricker sighed. ''Nothing, Mr. McGovern. Have some tea.''

CHAPTER 6

Java Sea, Morning, June 11, 1851

To Erica Rollin Rice her present position was a familiar one. She was sure she must have been born under an unlucky star. Or perhaps she was simply too immature and hasty in her decision making. Or then again, maybe she harbored an inaccurate perception of what adventuring ought to offer. Whatever the problem, she was doing something wrong. For every shining moment of these last few years she had suffered months of anguish.

She placed the napkins on the table and mentally counted items. What had she forgotten? *Butter*. From the little pantry locker she brought out the butter mold. Mold? The butter was formed into a simple hemisphere, the only shape it would hold in this tropical heat.

Captain Bricker came in the door, barely acknowledged her with a nod, and crossed to his desk to put his sextant away.

"Breakfast is ready, sir."

"Thank-you." His voice was cool, aloof. She wished she had the courage to throw something—preferably something very big and heavy.

Fisher breezed in with something heavy enough, but she couldn't throw the breakfast tray. Mr. McGovern trundled in behind him.

She smiled with what she thought to be a boyish grin. "Good morning, Mr. Fisher. You look cheerful enough today."

He handed her the tray of porridge and scones from the galley. "And why not? When I awoke this morning, I discovered meself is still alive. Reason enough to be 'appy, aye?"

"Aye, but if you ever wake up dead, you'll bound along for a fortnight before you realize the fact."

McGovern guffawed.

"Get on with ye, lad!" Fisher laughed. He gave Erica a friendly swat on the backside as she turned away, a jovial and innocent gesture.

She glanced at the captain as she entered the serving closet. He was standing there, livid at the intimacy, but unable to say a word.

Maude Harrington's door creaked open as the captain was about to sit down. She wore a clean dress and had pulled her hair back into a quiet, austere bun. Her eyes were puffy and red. "May I come out, please, Captain?"

"Yes. Good morning, Miss Harrington."

"Good morning." She stood there hesitant, as if such a brazen hussy would ever be uncertain of anything. She crossed to the captain and paused before saying, "I ask your forgiveness for my scene yesterday. I'm very, very sorry."

The captain held out his hand to her. "It was a trying situation. We were all upset. You're not only forgiven, the scene is forgotten. Will you join us for breakfast?"

She accepted his hand and turned to Fisher. "And you, Bosun. I wronged you so. Please accept my deepest apologies."

"Y'r lovely face makes apology unnecessary, milady, but I accept it all the same. And a gracious good mornin' to ye." He seated her beside him, across from the captain. Grudgingly, Erica put a place setting before her.

She looked up at Erica with wonderfully repentant eyes. "Eric, I apologize to you also. I hope I didn't hurt you."

"No, ma'am, you didn't." *Bite your tongue, Erica! This floozy certainly did hurt you. If it weren't for her, things would still be as they once were. And the pain is far from over.* Erica served Wun Lin's scones as soon as the captain had completed his morning prayer at table. Pointedly she placed the teapot on the captain's side of the table.

Miss Harrington patted her hair with both hands. "I had difficulty arranging my hair this morning—no hairbrushes. I trust I look presentable enough."

Fisher cooed something almost worshipful. Erica served the porridge, and it was all she could do to keep from dumping the boiling gruel in the Irishman's lap. *Disgusting it is, the way some men fawn all over women.*

"I owe you an explanation, Captain." Miss Harrington dug into her porridge hungrily.

"If explanations were money, I'd be a wealthy man when all that was owed was paid me." He was looking right at Erica. "Eric, is there any marmalade?"

"I think so, sir." Erica slunk off. So she could expect little potshots, eh? Very well—she could shoot, too.

Miss Harrington cleared her throat. "I wish I had some excuse for the fit I threw. I can't believe I did that. And after all you risked for me. You see, I find myself very anxious—more than nervous—terrified—when I'm confined in a small space. I can't ride in a closed carriage for more than a few blocks. I have trouble sleeping with bedcurtains drawn. When Mr. Fisher nailed that lid down—I can't tell you how terrified I felt. Panicked. I was trapped. I was reduced to such a wretched state I would gladly have given myself up just to get free of that barrel. But every time I took a deep breath to cry out, I gagged. When he finally let me out, I— I just— I'm so deeply ashamed.''

Fisher waggled his porridge spoon in the air. "DuPres's like that exactly, Cap'n. 'E's the best man aloft I've ever seen. Makes monkeys look like donkeys up there. But never send 'm below into a crowded lower 'old. 'E'll come popping out abovedecks like a champagne cork in two minutes flat, and shaking like a slack jibstay. Wild-eyed.''

The captain smiled at Miss Harrington. "If you're discussing some experience I should be familiar with, I must have forgotten it. I'm sorry. Old age, I guess; things of no consequence slip my mind.''

Erica clunked the marmalade on the table.

Maude smiled more than a smile. She radiated. She glowed. "You gentlemen are magnificent, all of you!" She reached for a hot scone. "For some reason that escapes me, there's a dress in my quarters all soiled. How does one go about handling laundry aboard ship?''

"Give it to Eric here. He's had some experience laundering dresses.''

Erica recognized the meaning. Potshot number two.

Fisher swallowed. "Aye, of course. 'Is sister's.''

Maude sipped her tea and laid her spoon down. "Are you familiar with the name Franz Bilderdijk?''

The captain nodded. "Wang See has mentioned him. Calls him 'that Dutchman.' I assume he's a Singapore businessman who drives a hard bargain.''

She made a derisive noise. "His public monopoly is shantung and brocade. No such fabrics leave the island until he's had his cut of their profits. And his private monopoly is, ah—'' She glanced at Eric. "Ladies. He controls all the gaming parlors and hotels frequented by Europeans. His influence extends throughout the Straits Settlements nearly to Australia. Perhaps farther."

"Sounds like a charming gentleman."

"I realize you're being sarcastic, but, yes, he is charming. He's handsome, suave, wealthy, and knows exactly how to impress a lady. He's also abusive, given to strong drink, sadistic, possessive. I could think of adjectives all morning if I cared to. I don't."

"And you're running away from him."

"Yes. Until I declared my freedom by boarding your ship, I belonged to him. Don't you see?" Her eyes locked onto the captain's. "By leaving his house, I openly defied him. He is not a man to let defiance go unpunished—not among his associates, his hired help or his women. There will be no mercy for me if I fall back into his clutches, and as I said, his clutches extend very far." She straightened. "But they don't extend to the New World."

"You're an American."

"Born in Chicago, yes. I have no idea what my status as a citizen is any more, but that's the least of my concerns."

Fisher wagged his head. "And that explains why the governor's militia could commandeer a merchantman just to search for a woman. Big money. Evensay a reward?"

The captain shot him a dirty look. "Mr. Fisher tends to relate much of life to pound notes, or whatever the local currency might be. Why didn't you tell me this before?"

"I was afraid you wouldn't risk it—meddling with the Dutchman. Besides, I've learned to trust no one—not his henchmen, not his associates, not even my so-called friends. I couldn't trust you, Captain, until you proved yourself yesterday."

"You took a big risk, not giving me better reason for hiding you."

The lovely shoulders heaved. "I knew what I wanted—what had to be—but not how to go about it exactly. Where was the line between saying too much and not saying enough? But I had to do something. Run. I couldn't take his infidelities and denigrations and—and he was so certain, so confident that I was trapped. His forever."

"You're still his by law regardless where you run. You referred to yourself as his woman. Are you legally married?"

Her voice was low and husky. "I've never married."

Fisher brightened perceptibly. The captain looked disappointed. Erica could have told him so. She had known from the beginning this woman was immoral. But on the other hand, if the bare facts of her own story were laid out, she would appear every bit as fallen as Maude.

Erica was not by choice immoral. She had been trapped, just like Maude claimed to be. She studied the woman's face in a new light. Was Maude as much a victim of circumstance—of men—as she herself? Apparently. She was a changed woman today. Either Maude Harrington was a consummate actress or finding someone to trust had shattered her façade of haughtiness.

Maude was continuing in a soft, feline voice. "I believed, too, that I was trapped. And I despised myself more every day. Then I learned you were about to sail. The Dutchman was outside town on the west end. It seemed the perfect opportunity. In fact, you were my only chance."

Her only chance. The captain had been Erica's only chance as well. Poor Captain Bricker—did he realize how many fallen women were clinging to him to escape their fates?

Captain Bricker buttered another scone. "How did you hear about us? We were in port less than a day altogether."

"Doctor Bigelow. He was treating me for a— ah— a

plantar wart. Not a very romantic malady. He mentioned in passing that a sea captain required a cabin boy; did I know of anyone appropriate? I didn't know any boys who might be interested, but when I heard you were sailing east—immediately I got the idea that—'' She frowned. ''What's wrong?''

Fisher and the Captain were staring at each other grimly.

''Would ye say,'' Fisher asked, ''that this Dutchman's the vindictive sort?''

''To say the least. And petty. Extremely petty. What are you two scowling about?''

The captain answered, ''Gideon.''

''Who is Gideon? Your sick cabin boy?'' She shook her head. ''Surely there's no way the Dutchman would connect me with him.''

''There are half a dozen ways. His man didn't find you, but the Dutchman suspects you're aboard this vessel. He knows *Arachne* and he knows my name. All he need learn is that *Arachne*'s cabin boy is in Singapore, and he could get that from Chow Chen, Wang See, the good doctor or anyone who saw me come ashore that night—and puts two and two together. Your Dutchman must have a thousand ears on the waterfront.''

McGovern grimaced. ''Wang See'd never sell the lad out.''

''Not intentionally. But perhaps inadvertently. Especially if he didn't know in time that the Dutchman is hoping for revenge against us. And I don't know a thing about Chow Chen. Gideon could go to the highest bidder.''

Erica refilled the teapot. ''Will that be all for now, sir?''

''I think so. You're excused.''

She tiptoed out the door and into bright morning air. The cabin air was so dark and heavy. No, the morning was not bright when she looked twice. The sky was overcast but not thickly enough to bring rain. The cloud cover made the water a bleak sort of gray, matching the gray sky. She looked aloft. In this light the sails appeared dirty; in sunlight they gleamed white as snow.

She wandered foreward to the foredeck railing. She stood with both feet on the cathead, the better to watch the white-water boil up along the prow. Nereids. Only now did she fully realize how much had slipped through her fingers. Her eyes burned hot and wet.

She thought of the captain's eyes that first night ever she saw him, anguished for the boy Gideon. And now Gideon might well lie in grave danger, and all because of that Maude. Erica's sympathy for Maude chilled again. And yet Maude couldn't help it. She had acted quickly and without thinking, exactly the way Erica had acted. If there were a victim here, it was not Maude or Erica or even that fevered little boy. It was Captain Bricker, who wanted only to do right before men and his God and to lean here on the rail, listening to His music.

Erica had lost interest in Nereids. She came down off the foredeck and ambled aft. As she passed near the mainmast she met the larboard watch; Edward the towhead, fifteen and lanky, draped casually over the port rail.

He grinned at Erica. "Hi, Eric."

"Hi, Edward."

"Hey, I'm off at sundown. Wanna play a couple hands? Cribbage maybe, or euchre?"

"Maybe." Erica shrugged and kept going.

Fisher and McGovern came out the stern cabin door, heads together in earnest conversation. She must go clear breakfast dishes away now. The captain emerged, but he didn't come foreward. He jogged up the steps to the far side of the quarterdeck and stood at the taffrail. He was watching the horizon behind them. He was looking toward Gideon.

She walked quickly, not to the cabin but up onto the quarterdeck. Quietly—but not too quietly—she leaned beside her captain at the taffrail. He made it plain he was ignoring her.

"You're still angry with me, aren't you?"

He shifted a little. "No. *Angry* isn't the word. I was never actually angry with you, as such."

"Then why so cold? Yesterday you were warm. Open. And now—what can I do to restore your good humor toward me?"

"Nothing. You are what you are and you can't change that." He looked at her for the first time that day. "A man earns respect by his conversation—that is, his walk through life. A woman deserves respect simply because she's a woman. Regardless this sham of yours, I do hold you in a certain degree of respect."

"And you didn't respect the person Eric?"

"Of course, but that was different. He was male, not much more than a child, really, just barely beginning his walk. Different."

"I'm not *that* old!"

"Neither are you Eric."

She was going to speak but she chewed her lip instead. She dwelt upon the marvelous camaraderie of yesterday. Without in any way compromising his authority as this ship's master, he had accepted her freely, held her in a kind of nonsexual affection. It was an uncle-nephew thing, a father-son thing. She relished those moments and savored them. She yearned for them and they were gone. He was now a gentleman, addressing a lady in the only way he knew.

Mentally she tried to restore that open feeling as she stood beside him. But camaraderie requires two participants and he was no longer participating. By "respect" the captain meant "cool reserve," the proper distance at which any proper gentleman held a lady—proper or not.

The full picture was unveiled, a picture spoiled past mending by Maude. She saw in the picture that what she yearned for and what she could achieve were two completely different things. Ah, well, she could cry over spilt milk (or beans, as the case may be), or she could continue her adventuring. Her impetuous nature had gotten her into this. It could get her out. Perhaps she could even make some amends for her contribution to this man's burdens.

"Uh—sir? It's true you can't take *Arachne* back to Singapore?"

"True. Not with Miss Harrington aboard. We're committed, now, to taking her on to safety. And there's still the goal of reaching New Zealand in time. Cargo is scarce and hard to find. If we don't take the load, it will go to some other vessel."

"But you can send me back. Call at the nearest port where I can find passage to Singapore, or flag some passing ship."

"I thought you wanted to continue serving here as you have been."

"I do! Even under the present conditions I'd much rather be here. But I can help you in Singapore. Consider: I know the city fairly well. I wouldn't be suspect, so to speak, to that Dutchman. I can spirit your little Gideon away and book passage to New Zealand or wherever. If he's too ill to travel, we can spend a few weeks in that little room I was renting. Don't you see? I'm the perfect person to go rescue your lad out from under that Dutchman's nose—before something terrible happens."

"And this is all your own idea."

"I think it's a magnificent idea. My dream back in Chelsea was to go adventuring. I see now that adventure doesn't come to one. It must be sought out—pursued. And the very best adventuring is one with high and noble purpose. Like rescuing a child." She expected him to brighten at least a little at the idea. Perhaps he would even see her sincerity and concern.

Instead, he both looked and sounded disgusted. "I realize it's the common province of women to be devious. But when you listen at the door, why not just come out and say you did? Why this blatant little fiction that you have a bold new idea? If you think you can handle the job better than Fisher, come right on out and say so."

"Fisher! What has he to do with this?"

He glared at her. "As if you didn't know. He's the one who came up with that idea. And I'll send him back to Singapore, not you. He's quick and clever—not that you aren't—but in a dangerous situation he can fight if running is impossible. He's a first-class barroom brawler. I used to count that against him, but it could work in our favor if he gets into a sticky situation. I'll give him all my contacts and he has quite a few of his own in the seamier establishments. Do you?"

"No, I'm sorry. I do not frequent seamy establishments. There is a line to be drawn when adventuring." She felt her anger bubbling to the surface. She should not talk back to the captain, but here it came pouring out. "I don't care if you are my captain; you shall hear this. I was being completely honest with you, sir. I did not listen at any door. I was up on the foredeck listening to your silly Nereids. And since you need proof now for whatever I say, ask Edward; he's larboard watch. The idea was wholly mine because I like you and I wanted to help you. I cared about you, but I see now that was foolishness. In return, the only thing you care about is looking and acting stuffy and proper. And I feel sorry for you, but not too sorry. After all, much of your anguish is of your own manufacture. Respect indeed!'' She turned on her heel and flounced off to the steps.

Difficult as it was to flounce when not wearing skirts, the whole scene gave her a perversely satisfying feeling. Maude was to blame in a way, but Captain Bricker was to blame in another way. *Men! Bah!*

CHAPTER 7

Java Sea, Mid-morning, June 11, 1851

The biggest problem in Erica's ill-starred marriage to Joshua Rice had been her temper. When she lost patience with a person (and especially a person she cared about), she became angry almost instantly. Obviously she hadn't changed a bit in that respect.

She roared into the stern cabin, fresh from her tangle with the starchy captain, and started scooping up porringers. She burned.

Maude Harrington still sat at the table. She folded her napkin. "Ah, there you are, Eric. My dress is in the corner of my room. See to it promptly."

"My pleasure. How many pieces would you like it returned in?"

"What!"

"And what color? The color of the slop spots or the color of the vomit spots? They won't wash out of that silk, you know, so we'll simply change the color of the rest of the dress to match. No matter, of course. Blue is blue. Let me know when you've decided." She carried her armload of dirty dishes to the closet.

"You just watch your impudence, young man!"

Erica returned to the table. "A word to the wise, madam: Haughtiness does not become you. Your mask of contrition looked much better." She snatched up the marmalade jar so carelessly she nearly spilled it.

Maude was glaring at her. The glare softened. "I apologized to you, you know. But I did treat you badly, so I apologize again. I think I may have somehow damaged your position with your captain."

"More than you'll ever know." Erica shook out the captain's napkins with a snap and tucked it in its ring. She looked at Maude. With puffy eyes and scant make-up, Maude looked almost human. "How did the Dutchman keep you, exactly?"

"That's none of your business, boy."

"I know it's not. But it's important to me for reasons you aren't aware of. You're a strong woman. You know how to get what you want and make demands. Why couldn't you just—well, assert yourself? Simply say to the Dutchman, 'That's enough of this nonsense. I'm leaving.'?"

Her laugh was abrasive. "You'll learn that life is never that simple."

"Oh, I've learned that much already." Erica sat down across from her, perched earnestly on the edge of the chair. "How could he coerce you so fearfully if you weren't tied by the marriage bond?"

"So you can trap some innocent little girl yourself when you grow up?" She studied Erica. "No, probably not. You just don't seem the type . . . Do you know if the captain keeps any whiskey around handy?"

"He doesn't approve of spirits. Fisher said so. But the crew gets their daily ration of rum—those who want it."

"Rum. Ugh!" She laughed, mirthless. "Why am I laughing? I might be reduced to that before this trip's over.

65

So you want to know how the Dutchman hangs onto his women. Pass the sugar.'' She poured another cup of tea.

"When you said 'trapped' it meant something to me,'' Erica said. ''My sister was trapped against her will. But the man literally kept her in chains. She could say 'I'm leaving' all she wanted, but she couldn't go anywhere.''

Maude snorted. ''The Dutchman's a little more subtle than that. You old enough to know what a paramour is?''

Erica considered a moment. ''I trust you understand that when I say 'yes' it doesn't mean I consort with them.''

Maude guffawed. ''You're gonna outtalk that glib-tongued Irishman if you don't watch it. Well, I was one for a while. How I got to the South Pacific is a long story. When I met the Dutchman I was doing all right in Macao, in the Portuguese quarter. But I wasn't happy; didn't like myself.'' Her face sobered. ''Know what really trapped me? My own dreams.''

"I don't follow.''

"Don't blame you. When I met the Dutchman at a New Year's Eve party, we liked each other and, lo and behold, he started courting me. I dreamed of being able to leave the past behind and begin life all over. Have genuine respect as the wife of a respected businessman. I think that's what got me in the end more than anything else.''

"You mean you let him court you and stayed with him, hoping that you'd have a respectable life eventually?''

"Something like that. And he's charming—a real heart-stealer. He seemed like he'd be the perfect husband—wealthy, well-thought-of, courteous.''

"Like Captain Bricker.''

"Your captain isn't wealthy.'' She smiled sadly. ''But then, wealth is the least of it, though it took me a long time to realize *that*. When the Dutchman invited me to Singapore, I couldn't say yes fast enough.''

"Did he forgive your past or did he ever learn of it?"

"I'm sure he must have known, but I never told him. I was afraid he'd drop me. Shoulda told him and I'd have been lucky if he did. How did he trap me?" She took a heavy draught of tea and stared glumly at the cup. "Just isn't the same without a shot of whiskey," she mumbled. "He trapped me by promising wonderful things. I sat around a long time waiting for them; hoping for them. He trapped me with pretty words. He said things I wanted to hear and I was afraid I'd never hear them if I weren't with him. He trapped me by being the most powerful man in Singapore, and that includes the governor. I couldn't say anything, do anything, go anywhere but that he heard about it. Every soul in Singapore's afraid of him."

"I see. Even if the Dutchman let you go, everyone in Singapore would be afraid to associate with you."

"Afraid the Dutchman might change his mind and want me back. Afraid I might be his spy. Your sister was lucky. Only *one* chain. I had hundreds."

"Didn't you ever love him?"

Maude drained her cup and stared morosely at the dregs. "Funny, isn't it? In a way I still do." She looked up at Erica. "And now you're going to go running straight to the captain with everything you just heard. Buy yourself back into his good graces with dirt about dear old Maude."

Erica shook her head and sat back. "No. No, you guessed right about the captain's opinion of me. Damaged past mending. Not just because of you. There's much more to it than that." She shrugged. "I'm very good at keeping secrets—mine and other people's."

"You? Secrets? You're not old enough to have secrets. Not big ones." She leaned forward toward Erica. "But you're still respectable. Hang onto that. I'd give anything—my life itself—to be considered respectable by polite society. And I shall, too." She sat back. "Tell me something. Yesterday when I lost my head the captain got howling angry, but he didn't hit me; didn't even try. And for some reason I never had the fear that he might, even though he was mad enough to breathe fire. Is he always that gentle?"

"I don't know; I guess so. I only just signed on this ship in Singapore."

"Really?" Maude frowned, perplexed. "You two seemed so close—so comfortable with each other, like you'd known each other a long time. You fit together so well I assumed either you were related to him or had worked here for years."

"Yes. We fit well together." Erica's loss welled up inside her anew.

"Your captain got a wife or girl friend or something?"

"He never mentioned any, but that doesn't mean much."

"No, he seems to play everything pretty close."

"I don't understand—"

"When he kisses, he doesn't tell."

"If you knew that, why'd you ask me?"

"Just checking. I like to know what I'm up against." She stood up and glared at Eric, instantly contemptuous. "When a lady stands up to leave, the gentleman stands up also, boy."

Erica shrugged. "You're no lady and I'm no gentleman." Little could Maude guess how true that was!

She smirked. "Brassy brat. See to my dress." She minced out the door, apparently dismissing the fact that she had just confided her most intimate secrets to a virtual stranger—and a young boy at that—for all she knew.

Erica could sense the woman's intentions and it enraged her. The position of captain's wife is a highly respectable one. Maude's claws were out; Erica just knew it.

She stood up and finished readying the table. *Men! Bah! And women! Double bah!* Erica wished she were quit of them both. She stopped suddenly in the midst of her busyness. Or did she wish that? Once she had sworn off men. But the captain haunted her. She was afraid he would succumb to the wiles of the likes of Maude Harrington. She was afraid he would find an attractive lady, perhaps someone who appreciated Handel oratorios, and—those eyes.

She marched on to the serving closet and stacked the dishes. No, she would forego men forever. They took so much pleasure and offered none in return. She had been badly used by them—well, by a few of them, and they were all alike.

Captain Bricker strode in the door and crossed to his desk. He pulled a chart and spread it out on the table. He stared at it a few seconds. "Eric, I need the chart that's in the pigeonhole immediately to the left of this one."

"The left. Aye, sir." Erica trotted over to the chart rack, the dozens of cells filled with dozens of protruding ends of rolled paper. How did he always know just which roll to choose? They looked exactly alike. A faint and distant bell was tinkling in her memory. What was it?

She pulled the chart from the cell to the left of the empty cell. Two heavy blue weights came, leaping and sliding, out of the roll of paper. One of them fell on her foot; the other clunked on the floor. Aha! Now she remembered.

The captain turned and frowned at her, irritated by the noise.

She picked up the two blue objects and waved them shoulder-high for him to see. "Maude Harrington's hairbrushes, sir."

CHAPTER 8

Java Sea, Evening, June 11, 1851

Erica hung up the dishtowel. She wiped the counter off and positioned the tall stool just so. Now what? She could look up Edward and play some cribbage. She could choose a book from the captain's shelf to read. She could wash Maude's dress again and hope more of the stains would come out—what a mess. Or she could just mope around on deck feeling sorry for herself.

Moping seemed by far the most attractive of her options. She left the serving closet, crossed through the dark, deserted stern cabin, and stepped out on deck.

The wind had shifted. Until now it had blown from behind, scooting them along. Now it came almost exactly out of the east, the direction in which they were headed. She could tell because the setting sun dipped low behind them, gilding the sails.

Crewmen were just finishing the onerous task of rearranging the sails. There was no doubt a word sailors used for the extreme angle at which these spars had been set, but Erica knew none of the terminology. But the sails were turned so far aside they nearly paralleled the sides of the ship. *Arachne* canted slightly aport.

Erica looked up behind her. At the quarterdeck rail the captain was watching his crew work. Beside him, Maude snuggled in close. Now and then he would point to something aloft. Obviously Maude was receiving detailed instruction about tacking against the wind. Occasionally she would also point or wave a hand. Erica simply couldn't believe her interest was genuine. At intervals she would look up at the captain with bovine eyes. Couldn't he see through her artifices? The whole sight made Erica angry and frustrated. No, it made her jealous. That was it and nothing less. The captain deserved far better than that harridan.

Erica turned her back on the lovely twosome and wended her way foreward. She stepped cautiously across a coil of rope too big to step around and continued on. Even ropes considered small on these ships were huge!

There stood Fisher and Mr. McGovern by the foremast. They were peering aloft, discussing some rope or sail. Mr. McGovern pointed and Fisher nodded earnestly. Erica paused beside a pile of rope and looked up, also. What did they see that absorbed them so? To her it all looked alike up there.

The second sail up on the foremast made a funny growling noise and began to flutter.

"Arrgh! There she goes, I bet!" McGovern wagged his head, grimly. "If she fouls the forecourse it's all gang topsail teery. Kelso! Grab the haly—"

With a mighty shuddering moan, the sail tore slowly and majestically from top to bottom. The ragged edges whipped backward; the ropes tied to them writhed, serpentine. Erica gazed fascinated. Everything aboard a ship operated on a grand scale, bigger than life, including the things that went wrong.

71

Mr. McGovern ran over next to Erica and began hauling vigorously on a line. The coil at her feet shrank as the line snaked up into the rigging. She watched entranced, as the torn topsail twitched downward inch by inch. Other seamen ran over to haul on selected lines, all a mystery to her.

Fisher shouted a warning. Something hard and scratchy seized her ankle. It couldn't be Fisher; he was over there and running this way. Her ankle was yanked up off the deck. She flailed her arms for balance. Her left leg jerked upward by degrees and flipped her toes-over-ears. Her head clunked against the hard teak decking. A careless shoe trod on her fingers. Two or three men yelled at each other.

Here was Fisher grabbing her around her body and lofting her high. She could neither see nor think. Fisher's arm wrapped tightly around her breast; did he notice that her body was softer than a boy's chest ought to be? He shifted her and jacked her higher. Rough hands tugged at the rope around her leg; her leg was free.

"I got 'm! All's well." Fisher toted her away bodily. He flipped her and clunked her bottomside-down on the forecastle steps. Surely he was angry with her, and Mr. McGovern must be enraged. Erica had disrupted their work at a moment when speed was essential. And soon her captain would come roaring over, angrier still.

But Mr. McGovern was shouting orders from behind the foremast as if nothing were wrong beyond the problem at hand. And Fisher's face was creased with genuine care and concern. He seemed not the least bit angry with her.

"'Ere, lad. Ye settling down some inside?"

She nodded. "I bumped my head."

"Aye, ye did. I 'eard the clunk so loud, meself thought we'd run aground a reef."

"What did I do?"

"Naething. Ye 'appened to be standing on the wrong coil

72

is all. A loop tightened around y'r leg. As the foretopsail came down, yerself went up. Why, 'ad we not decided to turn ye free, ye'd be 'anging like a 'aunch of beef from the topmast cap there.''

"Then I'm glad you decided to free me. But you shouldn't have. I messed things up royally with my carelessness."

"Fret not, lad. Things were messed up sufficient all by themselves. Topsail parted at exactly the wrong time. Let's see y'r leg there. Drop y'r drawers.''

"I'd rather not really." Instinctively Erica grabbed her pantwaist.

"Ah, that's right; captain mentioned it.'' He flicked his pocket knife open. "I'm gonna open y'r pants leg up along the seam there. Ye'll 'ave to sew it back together then, or else go through life with y'r pants flapping tag-end to the breeze.''

He slit the inseam up past her knee. She cringed; men simply do not do such things to women, and the fact that he was completely innocent of her gender did nothing for her discomfort.

He pressed his fingertips to her knee. "Bend. It 'urt?''

"No, not my knee." She flexed it up and down.

"Good. No need to work y'r ankle for me. 'Tis swelling up already. Begorra, what a beauty!''

He was right. The side of her left ankle was turning a greenish-blue color and rope burns drew sticky red lines around the bottom of her shin.

She licked her lips nervously. "You said the captain mentioned something about me. Mentioned what?''

"Naething much. He allows as 'ow ye feel a wee bit self-conscious about flaunting bare skin before the world. 'Tis natural; don't think a thing of it. When y'r old and 'ard calloused like meself, ye'll not think twice about letting the breeze kiss it all.''

"You're not old. You can't be thirty yet."

"Older'n y'rself, lad, and in more'n one way." He commenced twisting his kerchief into an elaborate wrap around her ankle. "Why, I bet y've not yet taken up with the ladies, aye?"

"Not yet." Erica felt her neck and cheeks turn red. She reminded herself that for all Fisher knew, he was engaging in sly conversation with a boy and would never speak so to a lady.

"Now there's something to do when we raise New Zealand. I know a charming little place a few blocks up from the waterfront. Not y'r usual den of thieves as caters to the seafaring class. Officers more'n common seamen gather there, quaff a cup 'r two, and there's some lovely ladies 'anging about. Ye'll be me guest."

"The captain go there, too?"

"Eh, nae. Lots of masters but not our captain. 'E goes with local businessmen to their clubs and such, but it's all very proper and hoity-toity. Fact is, 'e don't much associate with the ladies atall." Fisher frowned. "Doubt there's anything wrong with 'im, if ye catch me drift. Hit's just that 'is scruples keeps getting in the way of 'is pleasures."

Erica smiled. "And you never let scruples get in the way of your pleasures?"

Fisher chuckled. "Meself takes great pains to keep each in its proper place. Now stand on that. 'Ow's it feel?"

Erica came down off the steps, one-shoe-off-and-one-shoe-on. She walked, *click-bip*, *click-bip*, a few paces across the deck. "I'm sure it'll be fine, Mr. Fisher. Thank you very much."

"Eh, y're welcome, lad. It'll do till the captain sees it and wraps it up proper. Ye'd best support it for a few days till it mends."

"The captain has to see it?"

"Aye, 'e checks out all injuries and logs only the serious ones. Not this'n, likely. We'll not disturb 'im now, though. Saw 'im disappear into the stern cabin with the lady just before ye were wafted into the sky there."

"Oh. I don't think they are, uh—you know, uh—do you?"

"Likely not. But I'll not be taking any chance of popping in on 'em unannounced."

Here was one isolated instance where it was to Erica's advantage to appear the boy. Talking about man-things to a man, she could say things which under any other circumstance she could not—not politely.

"Does the captain have the first choice in such matters, so to speak?" she asked. "I mean—do you know what I mean?"

"Aye, I know, and the answer is aye. Y're speaking generally, I trust, of just any ship afloat and not just *Arachne*. Captain takes 'is choice of anything from victuals to company. Privilege of rank." Fisher studied the rigging aloft. The wayward sail had been gathered up against its spar but for one stubborn end. Of the four men standing in the footropes handling it, Erica recognized only DuPres.

Fisher looked down at her. "'Ere now, lad. Y're still shaking. Let's stop off at the galley for a spot of Wun Lin's toe-curling tea. 'Twon't cure what ails ye, but ye get so muckle worried that it might pickle y'r taste buds. Y'll forget all y'r other ills." He wrapped his arm around her shoulder and drew her against himself. Erica hobbled at his side, leaning into him, and his warm presence against her made her feel much better.

"Tell me something, Mr. Fisher."

"Fish. Friends call me Fish. Not in the captain's presence, understand, when we're being all formal and polite. But times like these, I'm plain old Fish."

"Very well. Tell me something, Fish. Are you considering courting Miss Harrington? I mean if the captain should decide he doesn't want her?"

His pleasant little chuckle rumbled. "Courtin' be not the exact word, since it suggests the 'ope of marriage at its end. Old Fish is not about to be bound down permanently to one lass. But if the lady mourns and languishes for a gentleman's company—and ye know me meaning—sure'n I'll consider it me duty to ease 'er pain, captain or no. 'Tis the least I can do for a lady of questionable associations. And a gorgeous one at that."

"What do you see in her exactly that appeals so?" Erica had often wondered that of men.

"Why the 'ole cut of 'er jib, lad. Fair skin, ample bosom, high-tone air, well-turned ankle—" He laughed. "I could do without 'er general temperament, which tends to being testy and short, but nobody's perfect, meself foremost. And in a lady that lovely 'tis an easy flaw to dismiss." His voice dropped a notch. "I'll wager from the words she knows that the Dutchman's not the only man what's 'eld 'er close. An encouraging observation, I daresay."

Erica almost revealed part of Maude's conversation and bit her lip just in time. That was privileged information, shared with her alone, though Fisher guessed it well enough.

They stepped into the smoky gloom of the galley. A single lantern swayed from the ceiling; the shadows on the walls pulsed and undulated. Wun Lin was hanging up the last of his copper pots.

"Tea, Wun lin?" Fisher grabbed Erica around the waist and perched her on the counter. He backed up to its edge and hopped up, sitting beside her.

"Tea. Yes. Rum?" asked Wun Lin.

"Why not, aye, lad?"

"No, thank-you," Erica put in hastily.

Wun Lin snickered pleasantly at some secret joke. He poured from a pot already prepared. Erica noticed his own half-empty cup on the other counter. He reached for the rum, but Fisher raised a hand with a "Don't bother."

From aloft, the lookout announced a ship in the distance. Mr. McGovern responded faintly and barked something about signaling.

"Ah!" Fisher tasted his unspiked tea. "May'ap that's me ride back to Singapore."

"How do you know it's not a ship headed in the same direction we are?"

"We're not about to go over'auling anyone with our fore topsail down. Nor would the mate 'ail a vessel going the wrong way."

Erica nodded. "I have a lot to learn. Including how to keep out of the way." She extended her hand. It held steady. "At least I've stopped shaking. I'm sorry. I wouldn't have thought being dumped upside down would put one off so."

"No need to apologize, lad. 'Ow were ye to know that coil was unwinding? Ye be a lubber yet, though I allow ye catch on remarkably fast. Won't be a lubber long." He gave her a brotherly hug.

At that very moment a shadow blanked out the open doorway. Captain Bricker stepped into the galley lamplight. "Wun Lin, would you—" He stopped cold and stared. Erica squirmed.

Fisher, of course, had no reason to squirm. His voice lilted cheerfully. "Join the party, Cap'n! We're celebrating the parting of the fore topsail. Young Eric must've appreciated 'ow we were bringing it down in a 'urry; 'e really got caught up in it." He laughed enthusiastically at his own wit. The captain was staring. Fisher's laugh died aborning.

"They're bending a new sail to it now, sir. Be in shape in no time. The lad 'ere tangled in a line and was swept off 'is feet. All's well now, as ye see."

The captain must have stood there for a count of twenty. He looked at Fisher, at Erica, at the kerchief around her sorry foot. Thrice he opened his mouth to speak and all three times shut it again.

His eyes finally met Erica's and stayed there. "Can you walk comfortably?"

"Aye, sir. No problem."

"Then bring a pot of tea back to the stern for Miss Harrington and myself. Fisher, we may have found your way west. Come with me." He wheeled and left.

Fisher stared after him. "Now what's all that, I wonder?"

"I don't know what it is." Erica hopped down off the counter. "But I know what I *wish* it were." She watched Wun Lin clap the lid on another steaming teapot. She remembered how it had bothered her when the captain and Maude stood so close together, arm pressed to arm. Wouldn't it be grand if he felt just as jealous when she and Fisher were pressed arm to arm?

But it would never be. She picked up the pot and limped out the door toward the stern cabin.

CHAPTER 9

Singapore, Evening, June 14, 1851

Seamus Fisher prided himself on many things and rightly
so. Most of all he prided himself upon his superlative skill at
creating opportunities where otherwise none existed. It was
a gift, this ability to find just the right happenstance at the
consummate moment. Unfortunately that moment was
eluding him; or perhaps the happenstance was out of joint.
He stood on the Singapore dock as life bustled about him,
stymied. He must find a vessel, any vessel, about to sail
east. Wind and currents favored passage north this time of
year. No one—not a solitary one—was considering an
eastward route.

Fisher's captain claimed the old Roman gods were mere
magnifications of human beings replete with the flaws,
whims, and foibles so common to humankind. Well, count
Lady Luck a member of that crew. She had bent over backward being kind to humble Bosun Fisher. Not twelve hours
after *Arachne*'s officers had discussed sending Fisher back
here, the wind had changed to speed passage west and the
captain had flagged down a willing vessel. Luck! Lady Luck

had wafted him here to Singapore about as swiftly as anyone could go that distance. And now apparently the Lady had traipsed off to parts unknown and left him standing here all alone, bereft of fortune. Or perhaps she was simply averting her petulant face, or turning her lovely back, showing her sloping alabaster shoulders. Lady Luck and Maude Harrington had much in common.

It would be dark in an hour or two and he'd been prowling these wharves for hours to no avail. Mayhap he should seek out young Gideon first. No, that would not do; some vessel going east, a vessel which up to now he had missed, might get underway in that brief hour when he was uptown. And once he had the sick lad, he wanted to be able to tuck him immediately into a comfortable berth.

Most of the square-riggers were now at his back. This end of the waterfront was where the junks tied up. He was not keen on booking passage in a vessel so ponderously slow. Aunt Fanny in her rowboat could overhaul a well-laden junk. Still, with Lady Luck in such a snit, he ought to wander through this end of the docks for lack of any better plan.

Within minutes he was awash in a sea of Oriental faces, all a handspan closer to the ground than his own. Here his captain had one on him. Bricker did not seem to note the color of a man, and he could count fast friends among three foreign races Fisher knew of. Fisher felt uncomfortable when his was the only European face in sight. He paused with unpainted warehouses to his left and slopping, fetid water to his right. He could smell both. He perched like a pelican upon a mooring post and pulled out his pipe and makings.

Here was another point of difference between himself and his captain. Bricker did not approve of alcohol and tobacco. A dull man in many ways was Captain Bricker, but an able

man, and fair. Fisher would cheerfully limit his use of tobacco to shore for the privilege of serving under him. Able
men and fair were hard to find among deepwater captains.

Fisher packed his pipe but he never got around to lighting
it. Ahead there, moored between two Foochow pole junks,
lolled a trim little red vessel with yellow poop and forecastle. He grinned to himself. A *lorcha*. The germ of an idea
planted itself in his mind. Even as he watched, three
Chinese seamen of disreputable appearance came off her.
Fisher pocketed his makings and followed them upstreet.

Lady Luck, who till this time had turned her darling
countenance away from him, gave him a broad smile, for
the three were entering a tavern known to him. The Palace
of Delight of Mai Foo See was known amongst Anglo seamen. He watched from the doorway until the three had
chosen their table, then walked to the bar.

Every female who worked in this tavern called herself
Mai Foo. Probably one of them was the Mai Foo of ownership, but just which was as closely-guarded a secret as the
whereabouts of the Ming treasure trove. Mai Foo the bartender looked up and smiled with teeth stained yellow by
betel nuts. "Ah! Feesher. You back so soon."

"Top of the evening, Celestial Lady. Might Mai Foo be
about? I'd be pleased to treat 'er to the beverage of 'er
choice."

Mai Foo studied him blankly.

Fisher held up a one-pound note. "Buy 'er a drink?"

"Ahhh!" The jaundiced smile returned. She grunted in
baritone like an overworked water buffalo.

From some dark corner the desired Mai Foo appeared.
She bowed respectfully. "Toppee dee evening, Meester
Feesher."

Fisher returned the bow and escorted her to the table next
to the three seamen. He hoped he could complete this ploy

before they decided to puff a little opium in the back room. Once they stood up, the game was lost. He seated his escort with her back to that table, enabling them to eavesdrop more successfully.

"May Foo, ye look exquisite this evening."

"Is that good?"

"As near perfect as mortals attain. Aye, very good."

She giggled.

"Meself was feeling low and I'd like to sit and talk a bit. Got the time?"

"Always time for Feesher."

"Bless ye." He sighed heavily. "Ever 'ave one of those—"

Mai Foo the bartender brought two glasses of something rather noxious-looking and took the pound note with her.

"—those days when what ye desire most just slips right through y'r fingers?"

She frowned a little. "Aye."

"That's me problem, right there. As ye well know, Delight of the Eye, the thing closest to me 'eart is money—save for y'rself, o' course. The king's coinage. The more, the merrier. And me captain, 'e just turned down the most splendid opportunity for making a very pretty penny, and all because 'e fears it might be just a wee bit illegal. Were it only 'is own pocket, I could see it. But it's all ours—the 'ole crew's. Sometimes meself feels like shipping out aboard some other tub, but I never seem to put me thoughts into action."

One of the three with his back to Fisher had been hunched over on his elbows. He was sitting up straight now. Lady Luck was smiling sweetly again.

"Awwww," Mai Foo purred. "Poor Feesher."

Fisher plunked both elbows on the table and cradled his chin in one hand. "And that's not the worst of it. Ye 'eard 'ow the Dutchman's looking for 'is lady, that—oh, what's 'er name—the one 'e commandeered the *Joseph Whidby* to go fetch.''

"Aye. I hear bout that. Many boats, all sorts boats go look for her."

Fisher smiled inwardly. He had suspected half the smugglers and brigands in Singapore would have gone off treasure hunting, and Mai Foo just confirmed it. "Aye. And the reward for 'er—''

"Beeg reward.''

"Aye. The captain would 'ave no part of that, either. Claimed 'e didn't want to get involved. Why, we 'ad as much chance of finding 'er as anyone. Though I admit this last is a richer prize by far than the Dutchman's lady.''

Mai Foo wagged her head. "Sad thing. You wanna come to back room, forget troubles, aye?''

"I'd love to, Lotus Flower on a Crystal Pool, but I've scant funds at the moment, being impecunious.'' He paused. Her face was blank. "No money.''

"Ah. So sad. Maybe you get pay soon.''

"Aye. Arrgh! 'Ow I'd love to be chasing after that prize!'' He sighed heavily again.

Behind Mai Foo the three men stood up. Were they leaving, or were they rising to the bait? If Lady Luck were grinning before, she was absolutely jubilant now. The tallest of the three, a tough-looking scoundrel with a red silk pillbox hat, mumbled two nasal syllables to Mai Foo.

She hopped to her feet and bowed deeply. These Orientals did know how to train up obediant women. "I must greet new customers now. Very good talk to you, Feesher. Come back, aye?''

"Aye, Mai Foo, and I appreciate y'r letting me unload.'' He paused. "Thanks for listening.''

"Ah.'' She bowed again. "Good day.''

"Good day, Jasmine Petal." Instantly he was surrounded by potentially lethal sailors of piratical persuasion. He nodded to the gentleman in the red hat. "Seamus Fisher at y'r service. Do sit down."

Stool legs grated and rattled as they sat. Fisher felt a bit more comfortable; at least they were eye-level now.

The red cap nodded. "Hwang Ahn. My compatriots." He waved a hand. "We did not intend to overhear. But we are at the next table, and to overhear was inevitable. We are distressed. A fellow man of the sea is distressed, and that distresses us. We would like perhaps to be of service. Is such possible?"

Fisher brightened a bit, then frowned, disconsolate. "Ah, thankee, no. Y'see—well—a junk just isn't fast enough. And we'd be quartering against the prevailing winds, which'd slow y'r junk even more. This project calls for a fast vessel. Fast and maneuverable."

"Faster than British frigate."

"Ye got the picture clearly, mate."

"Macao lorcha is fast enough?"

Fisher grinned brightly. "Now y'r talking! Ah, but what I 'ear, they were built for smoking out river pirates. Coastal trade at best. 'Ow does she do in deep water with that flat little bottom of 'ers? 'Ow does she wear in 'eavy seas?"

The man tipped his head. "We get there. You wish to sail east. She does well."

For the briefest moment Fisher feared this man knew too much. Then he realized that in mentioning quartering against prevailing winds, he had revealed his intended direction. He rubbed his chin. "And y're sure y're game for sticky business if need be?"

"Perhaps. We are, of course, law-abiding citizens."

"Of course, as is meself as well. 'Ere's the story in part. Understand I cannae give ye the 'ole of it. Briefly, a very wealthy businessman, a trader, from San Francisco was over on this side on business when 'e met a charming Portuguese lady. As it turns out, there was a boy child born of the, ah, friendship. Now the trader 'as died in Frisco and left no issue, save this one lad. If ye think the reward for the Dutchman's lady be 'andsome, ye should see what they're offering for the lad. Ye see, there's an un'oly fight over the estate. Some wants the boy found and others wants 'im destroyed. There be a big race on to locate 'im.'' Fisher leaned in closer. ''And I know where 'e is. But can I convince me captain to enter the race? 'Ardly.''

''Where would the lad be delivered?''

''Depends. The businessman's solicitor is sailing west from Frisco. With luck we might encounter 'im 'twixt 'ere and there; get a jump on the competition to boot. At the farthest, 'Onolulu. Possibly New Zealand. Most likely not that far.''

''To whom specifically?''

''Ah. That's me own bit of information. Sure'n ye understand.''

''And our portion?''

'''Alf and 'alf across the board.''

''We are nine and you are but one. One-tenth, each man.''

''But I know the lad's whereabouts and the contact to deliver 'im to. Tell ye what. One part for meself and three for the lot of ye. That's still five years' wages for meself and only a few months' work.''

They exchanged glances. The inscrutable faces were impossible to read.

''When do you wish to depart?''

''Sooner the better. I'd pick up the lad and we'd be on our way.''

''You would say, perhaps, that time is of the essence.''

85

"Took the words right out of me mouth."

The man stood up. "Join us. See where our vessel lies. Then bring your lad. We shall discuss specific amounts at our leisure as we sail east."

Fisher stood also. He extended his hand, a distinctly western gesture but one the man would understand. Hwang Ahn accepted it. Fisher bowed slightly just to top off the performance and followed the red cap out the door. Lady Luck was jumping up and down for joy.

CHAPTER 10

Singapore, Dusk, June 14, 1851

Dealing with the more polite and cultured European elements of Singapore was not one of Fisher's strengths. He vastly preferred the simpler life of a seaman along the waterfront. True, there were tricks to avoid being robbed or taken advantage of, but such were true in any area of living. Fisher knew most of the tricks for survival on the waterfront. He knew very little about the machinations of uptown business tycoons.

He stood now, scanning a row of British houses and feeling surprisingly ill at ease. In the half-light of dusk they all looked pretty much alike along here. There was the one he wanted—little brass name plate and a lion's head door knocker. He jogged up the stoop and slammed the knocker up and down.

A houseman answered the door. "Yes?"

"Seamus Fisher to see Dr. Bigelow, please. Important business."

"Very sorry. The doctor is not available at this time. You make an appointment, please."

Fisher heard Anglo voices in a distant room. "I'm just as sorry as y'rself, but me business cannae wait."

The door started to swing shut but Fisher countered it with his shoulder. It thumped to a standstill, and with his full weight behind it, opened. The housekeeper said something insistent, evensay impolite, but Fisher was past him and charging down the long dark hall toward the voices. This was it—this door here. He rapped once and entered.

Of the three men in the room, Fisher recognized the doctor from his captain's description. The second man was small and dark and square-built, probably half Malay. And the third stood nearly a head taller than Fisher and was twice as wide. He was a handsome cuss, nattily attired in the whitest of ruffled shirts, the trimmest of European-cut trousers complete with the stirrup to keep them taut, the latest cut of waistcoats and ties. His fair face was clean-shaven and framed by a mane of sandy hair. Even being found in a doctor's office, the fellow was the picture of robust health.

It dawned on Fisher just who this might be. He'd best confirm his guess anyway. He nodded toward the doctor. "Dr. Bigelow, good evening. And you, sir." He turned to the rosy-cheeked giant. "Might ye not be the gentleman they call the Dutchman, Franz Bilderdijk?"

The half-Malay stepped forward as the Dutchman looked at the doctor. "Do you wish him removed?"

Fisher talked fast. "Y're a legend in y'r own time and the talk of the wharves, sir, posting such an agreeable sum for the return of y'r mistress. She must be one magnificent woman."

The man's eyes burned into him. "She is my wife, not my mistress, and the mother of my three children."

"Oh? Well, ye know 'ow waterfront gossip distorts such things. Mr. Bilderdijk, sir, this is extremely important, though I cannae divulge why this moment. But be ye truly

88

married? Church wedding and all the legal trimmings?"

"Of course, truly married. Would I sire children by a harlot? What information do you haf about her? Why did you ask that?"

"I 'ave none, save what I've 'eard on the docks, and none of that concerning 'er whereabouts. Me captain's got 'igh scruples. 'E'd not bother seeking a mistress, but a mother with responsibilities—ah, that's another thing, regardless 'ow poorly she's been treated."

"You may tell your scrupulous captain she's been treated fairly and kindly. She is wearied of marriage; no excuse."

"I'll tell 'im that at me first opportunity, sir. And now, Doctor, I'd like to pay a brief visit to a lad in y'r care named Gideon. I sail shortly, so I've not much time, or I wouldn't bust in thusly. Just a minute with 'im, by y'r leave."

The doctor snorted. "You want to abduct him also, no doubt."

Fisher barely stopped himself from gaping. Abduct? How could this man have guessed? "Eh? Nae, not lest ye wish to be rid of the shaver."

The Dutchman planted himself directly in front of Fisher, towered over him, cast him in a broad and menacing shadow. "What's your business with the lad?"

Fisher kept his voice light and friendly. "A year ago I was in Praia—that'd be y'r Cape Verde Islands off Africa near—"

"I am familiar with Praia."

"Course ye are, sir. I met a lady there, a very proper lady, 'oo's little son ran off to sea. She described 'er boy in detail. The lad fits the description of a young tad shipped aboard a bark, *Arachne,* in Praia about that time. Now I 'ear that very lad's 'ere in Singapore, but I learned it almost too late. If indeed this be that widow's son, I can tell shortly by quizzing 'im. Does 'e by chance, Doctor, speak Portuguese?"

The doctor frowned at the Dutchman. "I used the boy three days ago to translate for me when a Portuguese sailor from Macao was brought in. He's fluent."

"Where is *Arachne* now? What is her destination?" The Dutchman could thunder like Vulcan when he wanted to intimidate a person. It worked, too.

Fisher shrugged amiably. "Gone, save for the lad, I 'ear. Me business is less with *Arachne* and more with the lad, so I asked not where she be bound."

The Dutchman's leonine head loomed above him. "Is there a reward for the boy, and who's offering it?"

"No reward I know about, sir. The lady's not wealthy. Me only return is in seeing the lad 'ome safe with 'is loving mother. Or at least telling 'er 'e's alive and well. Or recovering."

The Dutchman traded gazes with the doctor. He turned back to Fisher. "The lad is gone. Begone yourself, back to your ship before it sails. Go." Beyond him the half-Malay moved closer. If the Dutchman hired as a bodyguard a man half his own size, that man must be tougher than any three pirates plus a Sumo wrestler.

Fisher backed off. "Gone? On 'is own two feet?"

"Taken. So leave. I'm sorry, you've nothing here."

"Then I takes me leave. Y'r houseman'll see me to the door, I trust. No need to bother y'rself. Good evening, gentlemen, and me best wishes to you, Mr. Bilderdijk, in finding y'r lady safe."

The houseman held the door open. Fisher backed through it, nodded again and turned to step into the dark hallway. He did not look back, but he knew the half-Malay would be watching, for the door behind him didn't close until he had walked the length of the corridor.

The moment he heard the latch click, he flattened the houseman against the wall and grabbed an ear in each hand.

"Where's the lad? Speak quickly!"

"Taken. We don't know. Taken."

"By whom?" Fisher gave the ears the slightest twist.

"The Dutchman seeks him but a Chinese gentleman got him first. He came to visit the lad and, before we could stop him, he carried the lad away."

"The Chinaman's name, if ye wish any 'earing left."

The man's eyes bulged. "We don't know. We don't know."

He was telling the truth; Fisher could see that plainly enough. So a Chinaman had beaten the Dutchman to Gideon. In a false rage, well acted, Fisher stomped out the door.

Chinese, eh? Wang See or Chow Chen. Wang See was Captain Bricker's close friend and a wise and clever gentleman in the bargain. If he heard the Dutchman was seeking *Arachne,* and the reason, he might well have reasoned as Bricker had—that the Dutchman would use Gideon to reach Bricker, at the very least to work revenge. Fisher would call first upon Wang See. He took a few extra loops around the streets to make certain no one was following. Then he slipped around to the rear of Wang See's chandlery.

The store itself would be closed now, but lamplight drew feeble yellow lines down the wooden shutters in the back. Wang See was in his residence. Fisher knocked at the back door. A stifled cry from inside made the nape of Fisher's neck prickle. Politeness be hanged—he would barge in now and apologize later. For the second time that hour, he slammed his shoulder into a door. Fortunately, for his shoulder was getting a bit tender, this one opened easily.

Fisher knew this room. He had dined here before with his captain. Like any truly elegant Chinese home, this one was austere but for the gold leaf on the upright chests, plain but for the ornate wall hangings, and scrupulously clean. Mrs.

Wang, terrified, crouched in a corner. See, on his knees in the center of the room, looked composed and dignified despite his bloody nose. One of the biggest Orientals Fisher had ever seen brandished a cap-and-ball pistol; another toted Gideon like some sack of potatoes.

Gideon glanced over his shoulder and squealed, "Fisher!" He commenced squirming and flailing. He was a handful, even for so huge and brutish a thug.

Without thinking Fisher yanked his sheath knife. He held it wide, balanced lightly in his hand. "Gentlemen, and good evening to ye. I wager we're all after the same end: to return little Gideon 'ere to 'is rightful place, aye?"

Gideon's abductor took a step toward the door behind him. Fisher knew that door opened out into the store.

"No! Pray bide a moment, gents, and think: Ye got one shot in y'r pistol there and I got but one knife. Ye can drop me if ye 'it me just so, but I guarantee I'll take one of ye with me. I further guarantee I can pick off either one of ye without any chance of 'arm to the lad. Anyone care to challenge me assumption?" He looked from face to face. "'Ow much is the Dutchman paying for the tad? I'll double it."

Wang See climbed to his feet, a bit rocky. "I did not give the doctor my name. How did they find us?"

"Y're good friends with the captain. A thousand people 'ere on the wharves know that. They'd guess without thinking that y'r friendship with the captain might lead ye to protect 'is cabin boy. And we're mightily pleased ye did, See. But a few questions, a few loose tongues, and these rascals knew the very place to come, aye, lads? Now I've asked ye to be naming y'r price."

See wagged his head. "They are not for the reward itself, which is but twenty pounds sterling. They plan to hold the child for ransom, assuming he is worth more to the Dutchman than the reward would indicate."

"Ah. So the price is up. Well, then, gents, 'tis beyond me 'umble reach. Y'd best just take the lad and fly. 'Ere. Let me 'old the door for ye.'' He opened the door behind him and stepped aside.

The two started not for this back door but for the front door into the store, as Fisher had known they would. What he wanted was to be near enough the little charcoal brazier to grab a pot of hot whatever-it-was, and, stepping aside, did that. Taking his chances that his hand would be burned, he snatched the pot and flung it at the gun-wielder. The pistol blammed but the huge Chinaman's aim was spoiled. Mrs. Wang's shrieks broke the silence following the gun-shot, as Fisher lunged after the two.

Gideon's abductor made it out the door. Fisher snatched up an ornately carved teak armchair and heaved it. It caught the pistol-wielder behind the ear and helped him out the door considerably faster than he would otherwise have gone. Fisher jumped the falling miscreant and kept running.

The store was almost totally dark. Fisher knew his way around in here to some degree. Did the kidnapper? Apparently not—the fellow splacked into a stack of something. Oaken sponge pails went crashing. Fisher saw the abductor's silhouette in the gray-black of the doorway.

Gideon, bless the clever lad, was making life difficult for the man lugging him. He flexed his body violently back and forth. Suddenly he changed directions and threw his torso from side to side. His weight shifted his captor off balance, slowing the burly Oriental enough that Fisher could reach him.

Knowing his captain frowned upon antisocial acts such as murder, Fisher resisted the temptation to drive his knife between the villain's ribs. His free hand brushed a coil of rope in passing. He latched onto it. His grip almost failed; his hand pained him viciously because of the burns from that pot, but it held long enough to allow him to swing the coil. It caught Goliath in the side. Fisher punched wildly at the darkness, only half-aiming. Three or four half-effective blows are worth more in the long run than is one good swing that misses.

Gideon fell away and tumbled into the doorway. Fisher snatched the boy up and started running. He must stay on the main streets and resist the temptation to cut through alleys; he'd trip for certain over some fool thing left lying about.

Gideon clamped to him like an octopus. "I knew you'd find me, Fish. You 'n the captain."

Fisher gulped air. "Listen. No English. 'ere me? Ye—don't—don't speak English."

He was so winded when he reached the wharf he could not speak any language at all. By the time he stumbled drunkenly aboard the lorcha, his legs were rubber. A pirate rescued Gideon out of his arms lest he drop the boy after bringing him safe thus far. Gasping like a hounded fox, Fisher sprawled on his back on the deck and let himself pant and sweat and drift.

There was that old bromide about the frying pan and fire, and idle talk about rocks and hard places. This was it. If Lady Luck could keep her smile pasted on her lovely kisser a few days more, they would sail relatively clear of this dragnet of bandits seeking Maude and the lad. But now Fisher had willingly placed the boy and himself in the hands of pirates who would as soon feed them to the sharks as take a breath. He must thread his way carefully from this point on—very carefully indeed.

CHAPTER 11

Approaching Celebes, Afternoon, June 15, 1851

Erica gathered the last of the dishes from the noonday meal by stacking them up her arm. The fewer trips between table and serving closet, the better she liked it. She wasn't being overworked, nor was she genuinely weary. Far from it. The captain assigned her no job that might entail lifting or struggling. Her weariness was a sort of weariness with life in general, and she could not explain it.

She backed through the closet door and sloshed her dishes in the waiting dishwater. She wedged the door open with a spoon to better watch her captain. He was alone in the cabin, seated at his desk with his back to her. He had finished writing in the ship's log and now he was writing vigorously in his personal journal.

She would let the dishes soak a few minutes. She brought the steamy dishrag and a towel out to the table. She wiped it off and toweled it dry.

The captain must have eyes in the back of his head. Without glancing her way, he said, ''Thank-you, Eric,'' and abandoned his journal. He pulled a chart and brought it to the table.

Until that moment Erica had planned to go back to her dishes. Now she lingered beside the table. And when he rolled out his chart, she quickly and voluntarily held down one curling end.

"I bemoaned a general lack of knowledge about geography, do you remember?" she asked. "And you promised to show me where we were going—to tell me about the places we went."

He frowned. "I said that?"

She smiled and shrugged. "Something close to that."

He looked askance at her. "Well, this isn't the chart to show you on. We're still off it—somewhere out west of its left edge." He thumped the tabletop, then pointed to the map. "We'll enter the chart about here. This big round island is Borneo; and this spidery one, Celebes. Celebes is mountains and volcanoes and jungles, for the most part. Nearly the whole population lives along the coast. We're headed east, this direction."

"Why then we've very nearly crossed the Java Sea. Celebes is at its far eastern end, right?"

"Right; not so wonderful an accomplishment. The Java Sea isn't all that big, and we have had favorable winds much of the way."

"You said we're going to New Zealand. So we'll just sail right on between these islands here. Oh. That's Australia. North of Australia, then."

"Yes. Pretty much so." He measured with his two-pointed instrument (a caliper), not across the open sea space but to a dot on the long spider leg of the island he called Celebes.

She frowned suspiciously. "What's that dot?"

"The port of Macassar."

"What's there?"

"Oil. Know how all the young men in England slick their

hair back? They glue it down with Macassar oil."

"And we're stopping there."

"Just briefly."

"To bring all the young men in England more hair dressing?"

He kept his attentions pasted to the chart. "To put you ashore."

"To run an errand for you?"

"To find yourself another ship—another gullible dupe. It won't be easy; apparently I'm about as gullible a dupe as you'll find."

She sputtered, flabbergasted. "You can't do that to me! You said I could go all the way to England with you."

He snapped his caliper shut. "And you obtained that contract under false pretenses." He walked back to his desk to jot down meaningless numbers on a scrap of paper.

She urged her stunned feet into motion and parked herself as close as practical to him. "Please. I beg you to let me stay."

"The decision is made. I believe duties are waiting for you. You're dismissed."

You're dismissed. He said it so easily. He brushed past her and walked outside. Alone, Erica scuffed disconsolately back to the closet. *You're dismissed.* Wasn't that the truth! She grabbed the door and yanked it shut viciously. *Pung!* That spoon went flying against her ankle. She had forgotten the spoon. She picked it up. It was bent in half and twisted, a deformed, useless little Quasimodo of a spoon. Is this what Erica was, a useless parody of neither boy nor girl?

Tears were coming again. She wiped them away impatiently and plunged both hands in the hot, soapy water. If anyone besides Captain Bricker had dismissed her she wouldn't feel so bad. She could just picture the bouncing bosun letting her go—all apologetic. And the dour Mr.

McGovern would simply sound and act a little more solemn than usual. But the captain—she didn't want to leave this ship. No, being honest, she didn't want to leave the captain. She wished she could have admired Joshua Rice this much. She wished she could have enjoyed simply watching him do whatever he was doing, the way she enjoyed watching the captain.

The twisted spoon lay there forlornly. She wedged the handle into a drawer and tried to bend the bowl back up. Her fingers weren't strong enough. The spoon was ruined.

She was just as ruined. Her career as a boy was nearing its end and with this short hair she could hardly go back to being a girl.

She *could* explain short hair to the world by saying doctors had cut it during a severe illness. That sort of thing happened frequently and mysterious maladies abounded in this tropic corner of the earth. Perhaps if she looked more like the young lady she was, the captain would see her with new eyes. She had one skirt and blouse with her, jammed in the bottom of her duffle. She could—

Forget it! Erica told herself. *Both garments are shabby. They will never pass muster next to Maude Harrington's elegant silks.* In fact, the captain would never notice her at all so long as Maude hovered at his elbow. Maude was beautiful, well endowed, and totally feminine. Even in a skirt, Erica would still carry the vague odor of "cabin boy." Her slight build was neither well-endowed nor elegant, though people used to say she was pretty. No, so long as Maude provided a comparison, Erica could not hope to attract the captain.

Erica finished the last of the dishes and leaned on the countertop to think. Dare she "borrow" a dress from Maude? There were those five trunks, all unlocked, in the orlop. She ought to know. Yesterday, driven by curiosity, she had devised a story that Maude sent her there to fetch something (should anyone question her). That was just a story; in reality, she had wondered what could require five trunks.

One thing that Maude did *not* possess, she learned, was a gift for packing. She had thrown things in willy-nilly. Had she packed with care and planning, she could have come aboard with two trunks. And what she did possess was unexciting—clothes, some empty japanned boxes—not worth the effort or the risk of getting caught. And as Erica thought about it, none of the dresses was plain or simple enough to be altered to fit her. There were none she would want to borrow. Just as well. Even if Maude didn't realize whose dress it was, Erica's conscience would pain her. Pangs of conscience had made her stop snooping, halfway through the first trunk. *Bothersome things, consciences,* she thought, smiling ruefully.

Her duties were about done here. Should she wander about on deck awhile, perhaps to listen to the captain's Nereids? Neither the overcast sky nor the blustery wind would help her gray mood. Besides, the captain was out there. She felt uncomfortable being near him even as she longed to. *You're dismissed,* he had said.

Well, she was not about to spend the afternoon cowering in this stuffy little pantry. She had her hand on the door handle when she heard the stern cabin door open. The captain was coming in. He was laughing, a warm lilting chuckle as if he hadn't dismissed anyone for twenty years. Maude Harrington's giggle sounded, too. Erica waited, listening.

Maude cooed, "Well, I didn't know what to do. Fortunately some little old lady came waddling by. She bought the chicken from me on the spot and saved me no end of embarrassment. I'll never go near a market again, let alone nod my head.'' There was what sounded to Erica like a calculated silence. Maude spoke again. "Captain, I should think you'd get so lonely out here. I mean—you know— *lonely*. Were you ever married?"

Erica listened intently.

"Yes, some years ago in Maine. I was working coasting schooners between Vinalhaven and Philadelphia."

"Is she—did she—?"

"She died in childbirth."

"That's very sad. You know what's even sadder? That you never tried again; instead, you married yourself to this ship."

"It's a very pleasant ship. And as ships go, *Arachne*'s a charmer. Great character."

"You're playing at words with me, Captain. You know exactly what I mean and you're avoiding my whole intent."

He replied, but Erica was too angry to listen carefully. He was using that teasing tone of voice on Maude, the same he used with Erica when talking about Nereids and Neptune and all that. Maude didn't deserve his cleverness and attention—not in the slightest.

Both voices had dropped now to an intimate murmur and Erica could catch only occasional words. The foolish captain must have indeed spent his whole life at sea. A man who had any contact at all with women would see immediately what this siren was doing. She was blatantly, disgustingly obvious with her cooing and purring and soft velvet giggles.

But then perhaps he wasn't falling for her charms, after all. *Perhaps he was inviting them.* The thought shocked Erica at first, then angered her. Who was the seductress and who the seducer? If the captain were the moral paragon he thought himself to be, surely he would not condone this woman's wiles, let alone encourage them. But then, perhaps, he was blinded by having known love and then living years without it. Yet he mentioned escorting a lady to a concert in London. So he must have some experience resisting women's machinations—or inviting them.

Erica's thoughts turned ajumble, but they certainly were not favorably inclined toward this two-faced man, this animal typical of the species. She realized suddenly that complete silence reigned beyond the door. Had they left? No, for she had heard no door close. Then—

Whether the captain recognized a scheming woman when confronted by one or not, surely he must recognize when the situation had proceeded from words into action. By letting himself be allured by this floozy, he was as guilty of seduction as was that clever Maude. He was as guilty as every other man under God's blue sky. *Bah! Men! Triple bah!*

Erica opened the closet door carefully, ever so quietly, and peeked out to confirm her suspicions. The two were wrapped in a firm embrace, kissing, it seemed, with abject enthusiasm. It was a modest kiss as private kisses go, with no hands where they ought not be. Of course, all such kisses were surely precursors to less modest things to come in the immediate future. The fingertips of his left hand lightly massaged the bare nape of her neck. The neckline of this maroon brocade dress was exceptionally wide, and her milk-white shoulders curved toward him, around him.

Erica slammed the door as she came marching out. They both jumped a foot and disconnected instantly. It was comical, in a perverse way, but Erica was in no mood to laugh. She was so irate, so put out, her tongue stumbled.

"You—you two—you— Miss Harrington, you may have him!" She stormed out the cabin door.

CHAPTER 12

Entering Karimata Strait, After dark, June 16, 1851

Fisher had never before appreciated his captain's insistence against the use of tobacco in the stern cabin. Heaven forbid *Arachne*'s cabin should smell as foul as this lorcha's! Surrounded by Oriental seamen of half a dozen minor subraces, Fisher sat cross-legged on the floor. Hot, stagnant air hung heavy with acrid tobacco smoke and opium haze. Despite their sorry state, they were listening raptly to Fisher's performance.

He rapped on the deck with his left hand, then held it up as if it were speaking. "Innis! Be ye 'ome, lad?"

He held up his right hand and made his voice fainter. "Maybe. What ye want?"

After each exchange, Hwang Ahn interpreted.

Left hand: "We found a dory afloat with a dead body in it, about y'r size. Afraid it might be y'rself."

Right hand: "Oh? And what was it wearing?"

Left hand: "Checkered shirt and dungarees, high-top shoes, as me memory serves."

Fisher put an edge of worry to his voice. Right hand: "Checkered shirt, ye say. Be it a bright red check, or a bright blue check?"

Left hand: "Lest me memory fails, a bright blue check."

Now the voice was really worried. Right hand: "Blue. Be ye certain?"

Left hand: "Eh, nae. Wait. 'Twas a green check with little blue lines."

Fisher's voice crowed, awash with relief. Right hand: "Ah, saints be praised. 'Tweren't me."

Titters preceded uproarious laughter as the crew, one by one, caught the punch line. It was one of Fisher's favorite stories and he felt gratified that he'd gotten it across to these fellows of foreign mentality. But he was fast running out of jokes, stories, and anecdotes. Even his supply of war stories from far-flung ports and ocean storms was nearly dry.

He rubbed his hands together. "Gentlemen, entertaining as this little soiree may be, I'm about ready to call it a day." He translated for the translator: "Gonna go to bed."

A few sailors stood up and walked off or simply sagged forward, their thoughts turning inward.

Hwang nodded. "Very late. One thing before you go, Fisher."

"Aye?" Already halfway to his feet, he sat back down.

"We left Singapore in haste, without provisioning. Food is low. We must call at Batavia or Badjarmasin or Macassar."

"Make it Macassar; I've a friend or two there, can get a good deal on victuals."

Hwang nodded. "Satisfactory. Concerning the cost of provisions: We lacked time to trade, to sell, to otherwise earn the wherewithal to purchase supplies."

"I 'ear ye. I've got a wee bit with me, enough to stock on rice and beans and a pig or two."

Hwang smiled. "You are a most pleasant man to deal with. I appreciate this opportunity to know you and to be of service."

"No more than do I. Well, if that's all, a good night to ye."

He nodded. "Good night, Fisher."

Fisher stood and stretched. He'd best look in on young Gideon. He wandered to the far end of the deck cabin and pushed the light cotton curtain aside. Separated from the bustle of the main poop cabin by draperies, Gideon's bed seemed too small to hold a real person. Yet the boy was shorter than the pallet. Fisher could not imagine being this little, though of course at some time in his life he must have been. Somehow, as he charged through life, he always felt ten feet tall.

Gideon stirred in his sleep. Fisher sat on the edge of the pallet to listen to the boy's breathing for a few minutes. The movement awakened Gideon. The big eyes stared a few moments, blank, before the lad's brain made the connection.

"Fisher?" he whispered.

"Aye. Just checking." Fisher laid a hand across the lad's head—warm but not hot. He spoke louder. *"To eres awake'o. Como estas esta noche, Chiquito?"*

"Mejor, gracias." Gideon replied. He dropped his voice to a faint whisper. "Fisher, tha's not Portuguese. Tha's not even good Spanish."

Fisher grinned and whispered, "Good enough for the occasion. I'm 'oping our captain 'ere doesn't know Portuguese from Spanish anyway. Just ye remember, no English. Aye?"

Gideon nodded. "You know one of the sailors came by this afternoon. He speaks Portuguese real good. Guess he was checking to see if I really know the language."

"Mm. Guessed as much; shoulda warned ye."

Gideon grinned. "I played dumb and used my Cape Verde accent. He seemed happy."

"Ye're a clever lad. Keep it up." Fisher patted the boy's arm and stood up.

Gideon smiled. *"Bones noches."*

"Boneez nocheez," Fisher pushed back the curtain. He patted his pockets, located and dug out his makings, and headed for the forecastle, or what passed for a foredeck aboard a lorcha.

He greeted the larboard watch and climbed to where he could sit with his back against the foremast. Just above his head, the battened sail whispered. The moon was entering its third quarter; it hovered at water line and made sky and sea glow together, so that the line between air and water merged into a continuum reaching from here to heaven. Fisher rather enjoyed these moon-misted tropical nights.

Several thorny problems could stand the light of contemplation. Through no small fault of Fisher's, these cutthroats were now under the distinct impression that Gideon was worth five hundred pounds to someone. There was no way on this earth that Fisher or Bricker or any of Fisher's other friends could come up with five hundred pounds. But one could safely bet that these particular pipers would be paid.

Apparently these brigands had not heard that the Dutchman was offering a reward for the cabin boy from the *Arachne*. But they, along with the rest of the world no doubt, knew that the Dutchman was posting a reward for Maude Harrington. Wharf scuttlebutt tied Maude to the name *Arachne* and Fisher must assume these men were aware of that. Indeed, the Dutchman's interest in *Arachne* was such that a price might also rest upon the handsome and august head of the good Captain Bricker as well.

Now should Fisher by some miracle raise *Arachne* out here on these wet salt wastes, what convincing story could he possibly feed these lascars to convince them they should let him board her with Gideon? Any other ship would pose no problem; it would simply be the very one carrying that trader's solicitor from San Francisco. But the name *Arachne* was tied to the name Maude Harrington, a most suspicious circumstance.

And there was the matter of Mistress Harrington herself, not a problem so far as Fisher was concerned, but something to mull, nonetheless. The tone of the Dutchman's voice, and his indignation—his whole demeanor convinced Fisher that Maude was indeed his through legal matrimony. The captain was innocently abetting a runaway wife, albeit a woman of supremely appealing endowments who might conceivably feel burdened to be tied to the service of a single man for a whole lifetime. Fisher's memory lingered on her smooth white skin, the saucy curls (attractive even when laced with potato parings), the pouty mouth—he realized his thoughts were skating close to adultery and reluctantly shifted them onto other things.

On the northern horizon a red light gleamed faintly. *Arachne* was bound east, so that couldn't be her. In fact, Fisher held scant hope of catching them short of New Zealand and perhaps not even then. How he wished, though, that he could hail each passing vessel and confirm, for his own peace of mind, that he was not passing his own ship and master in the night.

This Java Sea was vast, but vaster still lay the South Pacific. And somewhere on that endless expanse, itself only partially charted, floated one tiny dot. *Arachne*. An infinitesimal speck bobbed on the biggest ocean in the world, and Fisher must somehow find it.

And that was the thorniest problem of all.

CHAPTER 13

Macassar, Late morning, June 18, 1851

Erica folded her oilskin jacket one more time. She shoved with all her might, hunching the jacket down into her duffle bag far enough that she could draw the string tight. She shouldered the bag and walked out on deck. The sky was still overcast, still sulking. She appreciated the mood.

Captain Bricker was coming down off the foredeck. She paused by the gangway to wait for him, and glanced back and up to the quarterdeck. Maude Harrington stood there. And her catty, smug look—the knowing, victorious look—made Erica wish dearly for a dagger or a sword or a gun or a cannon or perhaps a rocket sling of moderate size.

"Ready?" The captain started down the gangway without waiting for her reply. Disconsolate, she fell in beside him. They walked up a crowded little street. Were all South Seas ports like Macassar here—bustling, alien, huddled? He was walking briskly again, as he did when he was worried or upset. She was nearly jogging to keep up.

"Slow up, please, sir. Your legs are too long. Or perhaps mine are not quite long enough. Are you absolutely certain this is what must be?"

He slowed his pace to half. "I'm certain. I've studied this a great deal. I appreciate that you don't have to take my advice, but I'll give it to you, anyway. Address the world in your proper gender. If you're a woman, be a woman. Abandon this sinful theatric."

"'Sinful theatric,' you call it. You're being just a bit judgmental for one unfamiliar with the facts of the matter."

"It took me awhile to find the passage. It's buried in Deuteronomy. Verse 22:5. A woman who wears men's clothes, or a man who wears women's clothes—both are an abomination before God. If I'm being judgmental, I'm voicing God's opinion, not mine."

Here he was off on religion again. She had best change the subject. "I know I should have begged harder. When you hailed that ship and sent Fisher back to Singapore? It really should have been me. You need a bosun more than you need a cabin boy. Now you have no bosun and no cabin boy, either."

"I have Edward and Mr. McGovern, and I'll get by just fine." His voice was curt and cool.

She cast him a sidewise glance. "I know why you're doing this. You'll feel more comfortable about making time with that hussy if I'm out of the way. After all, who fancies chaperones popping out of closets! That's why you're dumping me. Oh, I admit she presents a perfect opportunity for a casual dalliance, and such things don't happen all that frequently. Why, I'd venture to say—"

"Belay that."

"No." She stopped suddenly in the middle of the street. "No, I think not. Since I am no longer in your employ you are no longer my captain, and I *shall* speak my mind. You are a worthy man in spite of your glaring shortcomings and you deserve better than that strumpet. She's as transparent as a crystal goblet and I don't understand why you can't see what she's doing. Notice I did not say 'trying to do.' *Doing*. And now you—"

"*Miss* Rollin. *Mrs*. Rice. Erica. Whatever you think your name is at the moment. Let me—" He paused and looked about. "We're in the wrong place. Come with me. And belay that constant blather." He took her arm, not as he would a woman's, but in the grip reserved for an errant schoolboy. He piloted her two blocks up a side street.

Erica would not have thought the exotic trade city of Macassar would boast a city park, but this seemed to be one. Rimmed all about with clustered shacks, a vast greensward stretched nearly a quarter mile. She realized from the variety and number of dungpiles that were she a farmer bringing her goat or carabao to town, she could graze it here. No matter, it was a pleasant place all the same. A clump of trees on a little copse studded its middle. The captain led her directly toward the copse. There the dense trees coupled with the overcast to make the shaded little hill a dark place indeed.

He released her arm and turned her to face him squarely. "I determined to dismiss you here in Macassar long before that, er, that incident. That had nothing to do with it."

"Miss Harrington thinks it does. You should have seen her face as I was leaving."

"I don't care what Miss Harrington thinks. Am I correct in this? That you picture me as some innocent babe being manipulated by a gold digger far more sophisticated than I?"

"Well, ah, I certainly wouldn't phrase it quite that way."

"Who is more acutely aware of unchaste women than a sailor? And I have been twenty-five years asea. Please give me credit for at least a modicum of discernment in such matters. But I'm not certain ab—"

"How old are you exactly?" she interrupted, frowning.

"Just short of thirty-four. I shipped aboard a packet as a cabin boy at age eight. But I'm not certain about you. Maude's kind I've seen before, but not yours. If you're spotless, why are you so reluctant to explain this strange impersonation?"

"For one thing, I didn't think you'd take me aboard if you knew all in advance. And in the past—" She bit her lip. She could not do it. "The past is dead."

"Your state now will be no worse than when you latched onto me in Singapore. And if you're escaping from someone, it may even be better."

"Escaping from whom?"

"I don't know. Maybe you're running away from this Mr. Rice just as Maude's trying to get away from the Dutchman."

"Joshua Rice died of malaria fourteen months ago."

"Then maybe you're looking for a husband of means. Rather than take Maude's route to that end, ship aboard as a boy. Look the officers over and make your choice. Then when you've sufficiently ingratiated yourself, unmask your little deception."

"How dare you think such a thing!"

"You see my three options? You're either soiled or running or headhunting. Any way it goes, you're trouble. I face enough troubles in the course of a voyage. I don't feel like volunteering for more by deliberately shipping trouble aboard. Rest assured, therefore, that Maude Harrington had nothing to do with this. I'm dismissing you strictly on your own merits—or lack of them."

"Merits! You speak of merits! I don't see you dismissing that harridan. If you're so resolute about avoiding trouble, she should be the first to go."

"She's a paying passenger."

"And I can just imagine her mode of payment." Erica

stopped. She may already have said too much. He looked enraged enough, insulted enough, to strike her.

But he did not. He did take several deep breaths, composing himself. She could watch the subtle changes in his face, the minuscule shifts in those fascinating sun-crinkles at the corners of his eyes. He did have a magnificently expressive and attractive face.

"I admit, I let her get a little ahead of me there, that one occasion. I wasn't thinking. I have no intention of taking immoral advantage of Miss Harrington."

Of course not, not at the moment. He keeps forgetting Maude Harrington can shape and change intentions. What about tomorrow and the next day and a week from now when her white shoulders and cheap perfume beckon to him in the lamplight? But Erica said none of that. To what use? Particularly, why should she care if he made a fool of himself before his God?

Perhaps that was it. Why did she so want him to look good in the eyes of his God? She did not care beans about gods, either his or Joshua's or, supposedly, hers. When she ought by all rights be very angry, she felt only confusion.

He spoke again, but his voice was softer. "I have to buy cargo, and I won't be selling anything in significant quantity until we enter the North Atlantic. So I don't have an excess of money. But I do have your wages here, fairly earned—" He pulled a fat envelope from his jacket pocket. "And a bonus. Your fine service earned that, also." He thrust the envelope into her hand.

She felt her eyes brimming. "I suppose it's only fair to remind you: You were to take my bill at Wang See's out of my wages. It doesn't look here that you did."

"I didn't forget. Consider it part of the bonus."

She was nearly whispering. "I'm pleased my service was satisfactory."

"I put a letter of recommendation in the envelope there. It may help you get a position if you decide to continue your charade."

"That's very good of you. Thank-you." She looked up into those wonderful warm deep eyes. "I hope Fisher is successful and they both rejoin you safely."

"If prayer carries any weight at all, they'll fly out on eagles' wings. I'll keep *you* in my prayers, too."

She could make no reply. She studied the front of the crackly yellow envelope.

"Well—" Did he seem reluctant to leave? It almost sounded so. "Uh, goodby Eric." He extended his hand in a gentleman's handshake.

She accepted it. She even found herself saying, "God be with you." She took a breath. "Now that was redundant. Of course He is. You're His person. Goodby, then."

"I hope sometime you become His person, also." He nodded, uncertain. "Godspeed." Suddenly he turned and walked out into the lighter gray beyond the shade. He hesitated halfway across the green. At its edge he stopped and turned to look at her another moment. Then he walked quickly off, swallowed by the crush of crowded, steep-roofed buildings.

Her brimming eyes overflowed; hot salt tears cascaded down her cheeks. Almost instantly her nose was running. That was what she hated most about crying, the runny nose. She fumbled for her handkerchief. She leaned against a tree a few minutes until the first rush of tears had abated. She blew and wiped her eyes. The crying was done. She must get on with life.

But why was she crying? Her mind buzzed in disarray. She must first get her thoughts in order. Clear thinking would follow from there. She remembered several signs in English and Dutch along a major street. She would find an accommodation, deposit her duffle, and take a long, brisk walk. Nothing clears mental cobwebs like a brisk walk.

Several hotels, some of them permanent-looking buildings, lined the main street. She chose one at random, took the smallest room available, and jammed her duffle bag beneath the tiny bed. She divided her money into four portions that she might seem only one-fourth as rich at any one time. Within half an hour she was on her way out of town along a narrow, rutted little dirt road.

See? She had walked less than three miles and she felt better already. The road, more a trail, wound along the flanks of a rather steep slope. But she could see nothing of the terrain. Dense forests and a thousand sorts of fronds hid the nature of the land. She heard the ocean off to her right from time to time, and gulls mewed everywhere. The trail apparently followed the coastline. She left the road along a faint path and walked down to the edge of the sea.

She found herself out on a point, a small headland that poked itself almost apologetically out of the forest wall. Working her way out onto the nethermost rocks, she sat down.

She could not see Macassar to her left, for the coast curved back. But a variety of ships, moored out from the city, lolled at anchor within view. There were several European square-riggers of one kind or another. A few small sampans bobbed about on the light swell, pretending they were not nearly as seaworthy as she knew them to be. The one really large native ship looked like a vessel built of odd parts from other boats. Its low deck houses were roofed with bamboo mats like the houses ashore. Its prow of unpainted shakes was narrow and pointy. Its stern, though, a hulking square box painted in bright red, green, and yellow, perched rather haphazardly up on the back.

Out on the open sea directly before her was a native boat,

coming in. Of plain wood, it was long and pointed at both ends, with none of this bright-stern nonsense. Its squarish sail looked ridiculously wide for the size of the vessel. And its deck house, too, was roofed with those reed mats. Gull-like, it soared gracefully shoreward. The sail spilled and it drifted the last few feet to a bobbing halt.

Only now did she notice its destination at her extreme left, a small village crouched on the thin line between green jungle and gray sea. All its houses perched on stilts at the water's edge, a full story above the restless surface. People in canoes commenced to go meet the huge gull.

These people were all happy. They had very little in a material way, and none of European comforts. But they were happy and Erica was not. She thought of the Malay and Chinese faces she had seen in Macassar, in Manila, in Singapore. They were open and cheerful and free of dark concerns. She was laden with dark concerns. The gull wallowed. Its two long spars swung slowly around until they nearly paralleled her keel line. They dropped lower by jerks. Nearly a dozen outriggers gathered around her now. Erica was too far away from them to hear voices or laughter, but she knew it was there. It was always there with these people.

But surely the same basic things happened to these people as to anyone else—births, deaths, illness. No doubt they fell in love just as intensely as any European and no doubt occasionally with the wrong person. Still they smiled.

Erica remembered smiling. Those first few months as Joshua's bride were all smiles. So was the first part of the voyage out of Chelsea and the last part of it as they neared Mindanao. And there was one other recent occasion when her heart smiled and sang—with Captain Bricker at the foredeck railing. Those moments, so few and so intense, were augmented by other moments here and there those first

114

days of her service. Put plainly, Captain Bricker made her feel good inside—very good.

Fine. That was established. Now why did he make her feel so good? True, he was attractive, as men go. But she liked to think she was not so shallow as to make appearances a decisive factor. He was strong—not just physically strong but morally strong, Maude Harrington notwithstanding. His strength lay with his God. He apparently subscribed to the same deity Joshua did, but the Captain's God was more a partner than a disciplinarian and taskmaster. He feared his God, but it was a wholesome, friendly fear. *Is there such a thing?* Perhaps she was thinking nonsense.

Erica went through the Bible verses she had grown up with, and the definitions she had memorized all those years, looking for a cogent description of Captain Bricker's God. *"Casting all your care upon Him for He careth for you. Be sober, be vigilant . . ." Peter something.* The captain was sober and vigilant, as was Joshua—well, most of the time. *"Ours is a God of mercy." "By the grace of God ye are saved." "For our God is a consuming fire." "Vengeance is mine, saith the Lord."* The more she tried to piece together the nature of God, the more any sensible description evaded her. She managed to confuse herself completely. She must get her mind off pigeon-holing God and tend to more mundane things, more fruitful endeavors—for instance, the reason she had broken down crying on that copse.

It could be that she had just lost, and she hated to lose at anything. She had lost to Maude in a big way. In a bigger way she had lost her fine plan for traveling to England, and it had been such a clever plan, too. Yet she was unmasked in half a week, thanks to that Maude. *Maude, Maude, Maude!* Why did that woman always insert herself in

Erica's life and thoughts? The upshot of it was that her act of whim—and that is what it was—had gone sour, and now she was pouting about it.

She might have been crying simply because she had enjoyed life aboard *Arachne*. It was a pleasant time she would never have again. That was worth shedding a tear right there.

She should start back soon. The sun would be down, quenched in the sea for another day, and darkness comes quickly in the tropics. She stood up, stretched, and worked her way back across the rocks. With difficulty she found the path to the main trail. It was almost dark already in these gloomy forests. She must hurry.

The road was heavily traveled now and she found herself moving against traffic. Constantly she had to pause and stand aside or else be trod upon. Guiding oxcarts, pushing handcarts, with bundles balanced on their heads, Malays of all sizes were returning home from a day at the market. They eyed her curiously, the young girls in particular. She realized belatedly that they were seeing her in her male *persona*. She was still not accustomed to being a young man.

She took in the sights and sounds and the feel of the warm, muggy air. She let her mind wander. And her mind, thus turned loose to follow its own paths, sorted out deep inside the facts she could not sort out on the surface of her thoughts. Her mind put two and two together, as it were, and summed them up:

Captain Bricker.

Love.

She stopped dead in the road as that summation struck her in all its enormity. She and her girlhood friends in the parish had discussed love a million times, though none of them knew the least thing about it. In the Bible and also in the

116

streets of England, men murdered for love. The love of Helen and Paris had started a whole war. Always she had looked at love as happening to others, never what it might feel like in the first person. *Well, Erica, this is it.*

She began walking again, rapidly. Of course he made her feel good every time he spoke to her. Of course his face and eyes—everything about him—fascinated her so that she never wanted to turn her eyes away from him. Of course she was concerned about his relationship with his God; that was of prime importance to him and, therefore, to her as well. Of course she detested Maude. Maude was not simply an unsavory person; she was a rival—a full-blown, uncompromising rival. Of course Erica cried when he walked away. The only man in her whole life who had never tried to exploit her in any way, the only man she had ever felt—well, this way—about, was dismissing himself from her.

She arrived back in town well after dark, outrageously hungry. The little stalls were all closed, as was the hotel's sleazy little dining room. She finally found an old lady down the street who was trying to sell the last of her *trepang*. Erica was so starved she easily forgot what live sea cucumbers look like. She found her hotel again with some difficulty.

It was too late to seek out *Arachne* tonight. She would return first thing tomorrow morning. She would lay out her past, her whole past—in as much detail as he cared to hear—before the captain. Then she would beg him, implore him, plead with him to take her back. Would he condemn her or forgive her? His was a God of mercy; she would point that out to him if need be. Perhaps he would forgive her. He seemed wise and fair enough. She did not care any more whether she would be Eric the cabin boy or Erica the cabin girl or simply another passenger.

She felt as happy as a Malay as she drifted off to sleep.

CHAPTER 14

Macassar, Morning, June 19, 1851

Erica stepped from musty gloom into cheerful morning sun and let the louvered hotel door swing shut behind her. Yesterday's clouds had dispersed, but for a pallid haze. She shouldered her ditty and marched with springing steps toward the waterfront.

She liked Macassar, at least more so than she had the preceding day. The sunshine showed it to be a rather bright little city—not nearly as dirty as some she'd been in, Singapore included. The houses with their steeply pitched thatched roofs were crowded shoulder-to-shoulder along the street. Almost every house boasted a little shop on its ground floor. The keepers, mostly Chinese, were rolling up the storefront shutters, preparing for this new business day.

The closer she got to the wharves, the more she worried. She had doubted a little, when she first awoke, that the captain would accept her story, her presence, and her apologies. She deliberately forced herself to dispel such doubts. He had forgiven Maude's outburst, had he not? But now that doubt and others were returning.

Most pressing of her worries was: *Have they left already?* The captain called this a brief stop and he had wasted no time leaving Singapore. Yet Mr. McGovern's first excursion ashore when they docked yesterday told the captain there was oil to lade, though not a lot. Surely the canny captain wouldn't turn down certain cargo, would he?

Also worrisome: *Can I find them again?* The waterfront was easy enough to reach. She simply walked downhill. But now she must sort through a forest of masts, a press of hulls. Tiny crafts of myriad sorts crouched among huge, stately junks and a few European vessels. She walked quickly along a dressed-stone pier, looking for anything familiar among the mélange of vessels beside her.

"Madam, please! The captain told ye to stay aboard!" That was Mr. McGovern's voice not far ahead, and he sounded exasperated. "Madam!"

Erica broke into a jog.

Here she came, down a familiar gangway. With her head high and her reticule on her arm, Maude flounced out across the pier in a swishy sky-blue dress—not the soiled one. How many did she own?

Selfishly Erica was glad the woman had gone. Now she could speak to the captain without fear of interruption or distraction. *Wait!* Erica paused to think. *Mr. McGovern could not come ashore to stop Maude. That means he is officer in charge aboard* Arachne *and that meant the captain himself was not on board.* Were the captain anywhere around, surely Mr. McGovern would have come blazing down the gangway to retrieve the errant Miss Harrington.

Erica couldn't talk to the captain now, anyway. On the other hand Mr. McGovern needed help. Already Maude had disappeared upstreet. By the time the first mate found someone below decks to follow her, she might be tucked away in some little shop, virtually unfindable. Erica would follow her, and when she saw an *Arachne* crewman coming, she would tell him where Maude was.

She broke into a run. Skirts were feminine and lovely and elegant, but when it came to running, boys' trousers were much easier to race in and didn't have to be hitched up. Already Mr. McGovern had left the railing in search of a crewman. Erica dropped her duffle on the wharf at the foot of the gangway and sprinted away upstreet.

She stopped in the middle of the narrow street. Maude was gone. No! There she was, just popping out of that little shop. The billowing blue skirt swayed as she turned and walked to another door close by. Erica moved closer. She looked all up and down the street and saw no familiar faces from *Arachne*.

Almost as quickly as she entered, Maude came out. She continued around the corner. She was certainly a hard shopper to please. Erica rounded the corner as Maude flounced into still another little shop. She moved in close to the door, curious as to what was so difficult to buy in Macassar. She could hear Maude's voice clearly.

"Cosmetics. You can't be entirely stupid. *Cos-met-ics!*"

A cheery little Chinese voice replied. "Aaah, yes, yes. Now I understand. No, no."

"What do you mean, no, no?"

"In all Macassar, no lady paint. No cosmetic."

"This whole sty of a town is nothing but shops. Surely some little hole-in-the-wall carries European goods of that sort."

The Chinese voice chose words carefully. "Seek. Go; seek. When you no find, come. I sell you this. Here. And this; see? Lady paint, no. These, yes. Many European lady come in, buy these. Make lady paint."

"You mean I must make my own?" Maude's voice was getting just a bit strident.

Erica grinned openly. So Maude had run out of cosmetics, and was desperate to buy more. Did that mean she was getting nowhere with the good captain? Erica most fervently hoped so. And now this little shopkeeper wanted to sell her, apparently, ingredients. Erica could just envision Miss Do-It-For-Me compounding her own powders and rouges. That would slow down her beauty campaign considerably. Erica almost giggled aloud.

"I can't believe this!" Maude fretted. "Oh, very well. I'm in a rush. I haven't time to go wandering all over, and the shops I stopped at thus far seem to agree with you. That and that and that; wrap them up."

"Very good, Miss. At once. Thank-you, Miss."

Erica could picture the gentleman's whole upper body, bobbing up and down in the unique Oriental half-bow, half-nod. Was that a secret to constant happiness—this exquisite politeness? She looked up and down the street and jogged to the corner to check the other street. Still she saw no sign of anyone she knew.

Should she reveal herself to Maude and cling closely, or simply follow from a distance? She saw no real advantage either way. What she wanted most was to be done with her completely, and here she was nursemaiding the woman. When her greatest desire was to explain her past and her actions to the captain, she was tagging along behind a spoiled, willful Jezebel. Ah, the ironies of life. Erica pressed back flat into a doorway.

In a complete grump, Maude appeared in the street. She glanced up and down, frowning. She started one way, paused, turned, and went the other way. Surely she couldn't be lost. Erica followed.

It occurred to Erica within a few minutes that she was not the only one following. Three men, who had simply been standing about idle on a street corner, were now walking along in Maude's wake on the other side of the street, moving at Maude's speed. They were mumbling together, nodding and smiling. Erica feared the look of them. All three were hideously unkempt—ragged, unwashed clothes on ragged, unwashed bodies. A white scar angled down the face of one of them; his sunken eyelid was sewed shut where the scar crossed his left eye. Another had no toes on his right foot. Erica noticed right away because, despite his mutilation, he was barefoot. Their bandannas probably had been brightly colored once, long ago.

Why would they want Maude? *That's silly, Erica. Of course you know why they want Maude. Yes, but could they possibly know she is Maude Harrington, and the Dutchman will pay well to get her back? Would the Dutchman pay to get her? Certainly, that's the way things get done in Southeast Asia.* Erica calculated briefly. *Arachne* had come directly from Singapore except for that half day while the Malay searched the ship and another three hours when Fisher transferred to the westbound vessel. But for those eight hours, *Arachne* was moving, and usually before a fair breeze. But then, any other vessel would be enjoying the same fair breeze. And the commandeered *Joseph Whidby* had overtaken *Arachne* in less than two days by crowding sail.

Were the Dutchman to spread the word on his waterfront that he wanted his lady, at least a few bored ship's masters would hear the huntsman's bugle and go off sniffing after the fox. And if such a vessel were to sail east to Macassar, it might easily have arrived within the last few days. Erica imagined idle ships and cutthroats swarming out from Singapore, if not east to Macassar, then surely north to Manila and Macao, to Brunei and Kuching, perhaps out to Vlaardingen and New Guinea. *Who knows how far the tentacles might extend?* A sudden jolt of fear pulsed through her. If the Dutchman were that powerful, not only Maude but the captain himself was in real danger.

No doubt she was overreacting. These three wretched thugs simply saw an unescorted white woman whose appearance suggested a dubious reputation. After all, a woman of unassailably spotless reputation would certainly be escorted. Erica moved in closer, and kept a close eye all about for any seaman from *Arachne*.

Totally unaware of the parade behind her, Maude paused, studied a little shop and disappeared inside. The three gathered at its door. They were certainly more than a little interested in her, all right. Erica walked on to the next corner and looked up and down. The cross street curved around the hill and she could see very little. She started back toward the shop.

Here came Maude, more put out than ever. The three surrounded her instantly. Erica was close enough now to see and hear well.

A burly churl with yellowed teeth smiled. "By some far stretch of the imagination, y'r name wouldn't be Maude 'Arrington, would it?"

She stared at him for only the slightest moment. "Not by any stretch of the imagination. Stand aside, sir." She started to move but they blocked her way.

"Then what might y'r name be, I be so bold t' ask?"

She did not hesitate. "Adrienne Bricker. I said stand aside." Again she tried to pass.

The scoundrel absolutely gloated. "Y' 'ear that, mates? Bricker is the very name we got an ear for."

"Ah, missy," purred the lout with the scar, "the Dutchman's not in the least gonna like the idea that y'r foolish captain's taken ye to wife."

"I have no concept what you're talking about, and you'll cease harrassing me or I shall call for the constabulary."

"Ah, the fine words ye know. Keen music to the ears of any edoocated man, I aver. Now open y'r sweet mouth with the least bit of noise and we deliver ye dead. The reward is very nearly as high and not worth the difference, I assure ye. Come along now, there's a good girl." The three bunched in close around her and began moving her by sheer force of bodies down the street toward Erica.

The horror—the abject terror—on Maude Harrington's face erased any hostile thoughts Erica had ever held against her. Panic-stricken herself, Erica looked wildly about.

There! Up the street two blocks behind them, a familiar dark jacket stepped into view from a cross street.

Erica began shrieking. "Captain! Here! Help! Here!"

The three blackguards stared at Erica confounded, then looked behind them. He heard! He was running this way! Maude twisted around to see and began screeching, also.

Maude should not have started shrieking. Erica saw the man with no toes pulling a dirk from a sheath on his belt. Whether they managed to keep her or not, they would not leave Maude behind alive. She ought to know that.

"No!" Erica must not stop to think or she would run away. Mindlessly she plunged forward and grabbed No Toes's arm. She twisted around, her back against him, and gripped that arm in both hands. Calloused fingers clamped across her face and gouged at her eyes. Erica was beginning to fathom the captain's understatement that she was no match for real pirates.

She stamped as hard as she could about where his left foot ought to be. She felt a crunchy pop beneath her heel. He howled; the fingers loosened. Prim and ladylike persons would never dream of hitting below the belt—of hitting at all, for that matter. This was no time to be prim and ladylike. Erica let go the knife-wielding arm, whirled, and swung her knee up. Her aim was satisfactory, but her legs were too short; she did not even half the damage she had hoped. It slowed No Toes to a temporary standstill, however. Erica grabbed his hand and tried to wrest the dirk away.

The group beyond No Toes exploded; the captain must have arrived. The dirk dropped. Erica scrambled for it but someone else's foot struck it, kicked it away. She could not see where it went amongst the tangle of struggling legs. Someone, purposely or not, whacked the side of her head. She felt herself rolling, falling. She tried to stand. The toeless foot lashed at her, caught her in the side and lifted her waist-high. She fell away, paralyzed.

The skirmish seemed remote, abstract. Erica wanted desperately to dive back into the fray, but her body refused to obey what her head instructed. She dragged herself to her knees; the dirt street wavered beneath her. She saw No Toes hobbling off down the hill, both arms wrapped around a wadded billow of blue. She must make sure the captain knew they were absconding with Maude!

She heard a hoarse cockney voice: "He's worth more alive!" The captain came hurtling backwards straight at her. She lost her balance ducking aside. Yellow Teeth, who moments ago grinned so gratuitously, was now snarling. He came roaring down upon the prostrate captain, swinging something, striking again and again. Erica stared, stunned. Her captain wasn't moving.

He had lost.

The third lubber grabbed handfuls of arm and coat and yanked. As if Captain Bricker were no more than a sack of rice, the huge man hoisted him to his shoulder and lumbered away. Erica saw now that Yellow Teeth had used an ungainly dueling pistol of some sort to strike the captain. He was pointing it now—not at Erica but upstreet. She lurched to her knees and twisted around to look. Two small Malays in European-style uniforms were speaking rapidly. They stopped simultaneously, frightened.

" 'Tis just a friendly little fight amongst fellow shipmates. Interfere and y'll regret it. Y' understand the queen's English?" Without taking his eyes off the two, Yellow Teeth scooped up the dirk and tucked it into his own belt. He grabbed Erica's wrist. "Ye'll do for an 'ostage, should I need one. Come along, lad," he yanked.

On her way to her feet, Erica bumped into Maude's parcel. It had burst open, no doubt trod upon. A pile of brilliant vermilion powder fairly glowed in the morning sun. Without realizing why, Erica snatched up a handful of the red dust.

With occasional glances over his shoulder, Yellow Teeth dragged her along. He did not really seem very interested in her, but seemed to be bringing her along more to tidy up the fight scene. His grip was so lax that if she twisted just now she could no doubt wrench free and duck away. And his dueling pistol, she knew, contained only one shot. He would surely not waste a bullet on a fleeing cabin boy when he might need it shortly in his own defense. But she did not struggle, and she could not imagine why she did not struggle. This was most unlike her—by nature she was a fighter.

She looked behind them. Not only were there no familiar faces in sight, the two constables had decided not to interfere. They stood in the distance watching, the cowardly clods. Only when she noticed splotches of red on the ground did she realize the vermilion powder was leaking from her clenched fist. From that point on she trickled vermilion through her fingers in niggardly amounts. She ran out of powder at the gangway of the cutthroats' ship.

CHAPTER 15

Noon, June 19, 1851

There is darkness and there is blackness, Erica mused. This was blackness wherein no light gleamed, no star twinkled, no gray smudge promised more light to come. "Black as a ship's hold" was more than just an adage. She abhorred sitting in this ship's hold now in such utter, abject blackness.

The weight in her lap moved slightly. Her captain was waking up again. She took the opportunity to raise herself from the floor and flex her sore backside muscles. She felt numb from sitting motionless on the deck planking so long. She settled down again and leaned back against the rough boards.

She groped for his collarbone, and from there, ran her fingers up the side of his face to his temple. Still sticky, but not wet—the bleeding had stopped.

He took a deep breath and muttered something she could not quite catch.

She followed his shoulder and arm down to his hand, checking. The fingers were still clammy cold, as they had been. But they turned now and wrapped around hers. He held on for several minutes.

The hold here was so silent that her whispers sounded like shouts. She kept her voice very low, though there was no one else to hear. "I'm not going to ask you how you feel. I think I have a general notion."

"Eric?"

"Very good, sir."

"Did they catch Miss Harrington? Could she get away?"

"They did and she couldn't. I suspect at least one of them kept a good tight grip on her the whole fight, though I couldn't see. She certainly tried to free herself—struggling, squirming, shrieking like a banshee."

"Where is she? I don't hear her."

"Nor will you. I would imagine she's up in the stern cabin with the other elite of this scow. Her proper place. They didn't throw her in this hold at any rate."

"How long have we been down here?"

"I've been wondering about that. No more than two hours, I suppose. But it seems much longer. You started to wake up once but it didn't last. They brought us aboard immediately after that little brouhaha. And you can't believe how terribly delighted they all were to see the two of you. I gather they hope to turn a handsome profit by dragging you two back to Singapore. They emptied your pockets—had to make sure you were the captain in question. Took your matches, I gather so you can't burn up their ship. And they took that pretty little pocket knife.

"And they made all these, well, ugly comments. Incidentally Maude tried to talk her way out by claiming to be Mrs. Bricker. I don't think that will help your cause much. I was snuffling a little. I felt very low, as you may well imagine. Some smelly person with a tooth missing in front jabbed my arm like this—" she demonstrated gently

"—and said 'Stop y'r sniveling. Be a man!' Fat lot he knows. They were getting underway even while all this was going on. In a muckle rush they were."

"Mmmm." Another deep sigh. Was he drifting off again or struggling to return to something of his usual alertness? Perhaps she'd better keep him talking.

"You were going to look for oil to round out your cargo. Did you find any?"

"No." He paused, then amended his answer. "No, I didn't look for oil, and, no, I didn't find any."

"What did you do all the rest of yesterday, then? And this morning. You weren't aboard this morning, were you?"

"I was looking for you."

"Really! Should I be flattered?"

"I hope so. I worked for days to convince myself that dismissing you was the best thing to do. But when I got back to *Arachne*—sat down in my chair—you weren't in the pantry, you weren't bouncing around anywhere; I knew then it was a terrible mistake. But you left the green before I got back there. I looked everywhere in the city for you. It was as though you'd evaporated."

"I went for a walk. So sorry I missed you. I had a great deal of thinking to do, as you can understand, and I needed some solitude. What is a rather long ship that's thin and barren-looking in front and square and brightly painted in back?"

"A prau. I've heard them called flying praus, too. Usually pirate vessels, usually well armed. Where'd you see it?"

"Tied out from the city a ways. And what is a ship, long and thin at both ends with an absolutely enormous sail? Local design, I should guess."

"One mast with a very wide spar? Caracor. Has an outrigger."

129

"That's it. It put in at a little village as I watched. Have you ever noted how happy these Malays are? The villagers and all?"

"Uh-huh." He sounded more as though he were talking to Eric than to Erica. Despite their position, she felt elated. On the other hand, he didn't sound interested in the fine points of local shipping or the joys of being a Malay.

To use a nautical phrase, she took a different tack. "Do you remember when you first discovered my, ah, secret and you said you felt betrayed because I had brightened your voyage? Is that accurate?"

"That's pretty accurate."

"And then you said 'I'm sorry you are what you are. I liked Eric very much.'"

"I don't remember my exact words. That was my feeling at the time, though."

"Eric isn't gone, you know. He never left. I didn't change. Do you realize that, in fact, you called me Eric a few minutes ago when you weren't really all that awake yet? The person you explained the Nereids to is the selfsame person you confronted in the serving closet. I am me. And once upon a time you seemed to like me very much. Do you understand what I'm trying to say?"

"Yes. I do." He heaved another of those heavy sighs. His head must be throbbing terribly. Suddenly he turned to face her, though of course no one could see anything in this blackness. "How thoughtless can I be? You were in the thick of the fight. Are you hurt?"

"No. Not really. A couple of bumps, a thump in the side. No blood spilt, which is more than you can say. He beat on your poor head with a dueling pistol. Did you know that?"

"He was going to fire the ball into my belly and not a thing I could do to stop him. But his chum yelled something."

130

"I believe he said something to the effect that you're worth more alive than dead."

"Wonderful." His voice dripped bitterness. It softened. "You're sure you're not hurt at all?"

"Quite certain. Thank-you. Of course, that is in reference to the immediate effects of the skirmish. Excuse my saying so, but my posterior aspect is in disastrous straits at the moment. I'm afraid I really must move, at least for a minute or two. Here." She pulled off her cutaway jacket and waistcoat. She rolled them into a loose wad to pillow his head. She wiggled out from under him and tucked the roll where her lap had been. "Is that all right for you?"

"Fine. It's—what is it, your jacket?"

She might as well have a bit of fun with this. "Jacket and shirt and all. We must keep you comfortable, musn't we?"

"Your shirt and—now, look! Just because it's dark—"

"It's absolutely pure, pitch, Stygian black and who's to know?" She giggled. "However, I overstated slightly. It's the jacket and waistcoat only. Your propriety is preserved."

Was he angry? She couldn't tell. When he spoke she knew he wasn't. His voice had regained something of that lilt she had liked so much that day on the foredeck. He was feeling better. "You obviously weren't spanked enough when you were young. You don't have an ounce of respect for man or beast or moral law."

"Respect? I certainly have. But I remember more than once you took devilish delight in teasing. Sauce for the goose and all that." She mused a few moments. "On second thought, perhaps you're absolutely right. I at least lack the respect to hold my peace just now, but I'm too anxious to know: After you dismissed me, did Maude, ah, approach you, and did you rebuff her advances? Not just yesterday, but before that, too."

"Why do you ask?"

"She came ashore to buy cosmetics, which led me to deduce that (a) her supply was becoming exhausted and (b) she felt the need of additional ammunition in her fight to win you. I suppose *seduce* is a closer term than *win*."

He chuckled, that loose and rippling laugh. She could just imagine his sun-crinkles bunching up. "Very shrewd of you. That painful incident, when you came clanging out of the serving closet like a blamed jack-in-the-box, served one good purpose. It reminded me, speaking frankly, of my fleshly responsibility toward my Lord. It reminded me to put my guard back up. She tried half a dozen times to pick up again where we left off. She's a most enticing woman."

"I think I can understand at least a little the temptation. Not only beautiful but willing and, ah, shall we say knowledgeable in the ways of pleasing a man?"

"I think we could say that. Yes, a temptation. And you were right about her thinking that incident was the reason you were fired. Then after I put you ashore and returned, she said something to the effect that now our blankety-blank chaperone is gone, let's get to know one another better. Those weren't her exact words; I'm very poor at repeating exact quotes, and that includes Scripture verses. But you get the idea."

"Clearly. Funny. I would never have guessed anything good at all could come of that—what you called a painful incident."

"I suppose the standard cliché applies here: The Lord works in mysterious ways."

He was silent a few minutes.

She walked in tight little circles, stretching her stiff limbs and rubbing her aching backside.

His voice came so suddenly in the silence it startled her. "You said, as I recall, that perhaps you might explain yourself sometime. Is this the time?"

"It's half a day past time. When I saw Maude coming down your gangway, I was on my way to you to tell you everything, beg your forgiveness, and entreat you to take me back. Had you been available, and had Maude not gone cavorting off, you would have heard the whole story hours ago."

"Start by sorting the fact from the fiction. Were your parents actually missionaries?"

"Yes. But they were not serving here in the Orient when I was born. They had returned to their parish in Chelsea. I was born in England. The part that they died untimely is true also. Smallpox. I was thirteen. The vicar made me a ward of the parish. I worked as a sort of charwoman in return for keep and some education. It was a rather nice arrangement, now I look back, but at the time I loathed it."

"Cleaning? That kind of thing?"

"Helping the regular charwoman. Cleaning the brass and silver in the sanctuary, washing the vicar's vestments, pulling weeds in the garden out back, rubbing out the initials small boys carved in the choir loft. Such chores as that."

"Joshua Rice came to the vicar when I was seventeen—just barely seventeen—and wanted to train for the mission field. He was intensely dedicated and eager to go. He was pleasant, polite, well-behaved; the vicar liked him. So did I. When someone suggested a married man would be more appropriate in the field, so to speak, the idea just sort of fell together that I would marry him and we'd both go."

"That was all there was to it? I mean—no love?"

"What did I know about love? He was scrawny but rather attractive, and I liked him. I was looking for no more than that. I suspect now I was in love most of all with the chance to get out of the vicarage. No more dull, dreary toil in a

133

dull, dreary place. Chelsea is what you'd call drab under the best of circumstances. I wanted to see exotic places like my parents had. Go adventuring. You know—*do* things. I mean, things besides polishing four-hundred-year-old candlesticks.''

"At eighteen."

''Yes. The voyage to Manila was our honeymoon cruise.''

"Very romantic."

She licked her lips. ''Since you were speaking frankly in reference to Miss Harrington, I shall also. Neither Joshua nor I had the least notion of what married couples, uh, do. We weren't even certain whether anything is permissible or if sin began where good behavior left off. And besides, there are many other difficult aspects to marriage—molding your life to that of another when you're both of independent spirit. Oh, we would have succeeded in marriage. We were both determined enough.''

He rustled in the blackness.

''Are you getting up? You shouldn't, you know.''

''Just sitting. I'm all right. Keep going.''

''Well, the end of it is, I have a much healthier respect for how much marriage requires of one. I've lost my casual attitude toward it.''

''And you say he died of malaria?''

''A fortnight before our boat was to sail from Manila to China. We spent some months in Manila learning Chinese. Well, he learned Chinese. I never did get the hang of it; the words all sounded alike to me. Anyway, suddenly he was gone. I had a little money but not enough to get back to England. I didn't know what to do. The local church was very poor. They couldn't really help. And with my background I was dreadfully afraid to ask them; to even speak to them. Anglicans and Romans—Henry the Eighth and the

Pope—you know. So foolish of me. I see that now.

"Obviously the thing to do was earn enough money to get back to England—or perhaps America or Canada. A man offered to hire me as a maid and nanny. He was Spanish, smaller than you, and very dark-complexioned. He gave me his address so I could come be interviewed by his wife. Well, when I got there, I found there was no wife and he, ah—" Here it came. Here it all came and Erica just knew it would shatter the fragile rapport they had established in this black hold. "He, ah, intended to violate me. Keep me. He said so in so many words, and he threatened me great harm if I should tell a soul. I couldn't fight him, so I pretended to be amenable to the idea. I suggested that I would step in the next room and disrobe. Oh, he liked the idea! So I stepped into the other room and out the second-story window, worked my way down the tile roof to some gnarled sort of tree, climbed to the ground, and ran home. I abandoned the apartment quickly lest he come find me."

He was chuckling. "I can just picture that, knowing you."

Erica frowned. He could afford to chuckle. The worst was yet to come. "Then I met this nice man, an older man, a man of means. He was a trader and ship's master, just like you. He offered to take me back to England. By now, you see, I was all for going home to England. I'd pick up again at the vicarage, find some nice young man with a farm, get married, and forget this ridiculous urge for adventure. The shipmaster would give me cabin space, he said. He rather intimated it would be a service to the church."

"What's his name?"

"Abram Sykes, *Cartagena*. Do you know him?"

"I met him once." His voice sounded subdued. "Let me second-guess your story. His free offer had strings attached."

"That's putting it nicely, to say the least. He had no intention of sailing anywhere near England. Almost a year later we were still in the South Seas. He chained me to his bunk whenever we were in port and only let me out of the cabin if he was with me. That's slavery, you know."

"Given to drink? Captain Sykes, I mean."

"Only one of many vices." She sat down carefully nearby, she hoped. "How close am I to you?"

"Oh, about this close."

"Very funny." But his voice had given her a more precise fix. She wriggled in a bit closer. Her foot bumped against her discarded jacket and vest, and since he wasn't using them, she put them back on. "There was one young man, his seaman. I found him alone on one occasion and begged him to help me. He seemed such a decent sort and sympathetic to my plight. But he wouldn't help. He said the captain's business was the captain's business and he wouldn't interfere. The captain was master."

"That's right. Not a man among them would have lifted a finger for you, no matter how much they'd like to. Calling the captain on a moral issue is as much mutiny as calling him on a point of authority."

She buttoned her waistcoat. "Then Miss Harrington posed a far greater temptation than I suspected. You mean you could have done anything you wished? And the crew would simply turn their faces away?"

"Anything I wanted. Nobody's business but my own. And God's, of course, but that too is my own affair, not the crew's."

"Of course." There he was again, on religion. Yet the tone of his voice was not one of fearing God's wrath but rather one of fearing disappointing Him. It was a fine line, but clear. Curious. She must ask him about it. "We were coming into Singapore a few weeks before I met you,"

136

Erica continued. "There are those outer islands, you know, off to the left of the ship as you're coming around from Malacca. Anyway, I saw we'd pass rather close and he hadn't chained me up yet. So I gathered a change of clothes into a bundle, and stripped to my unmentionables. I broke up a locker door and squeezed both it and me out the port-hole. I don't know what I would've done had I got stuck halfway—or what he would've done, for that. It was late evening, nearly dark. If the watch saw me they didn't say anything. I kicked and floated ashore on the broken-up wood."

"God was good to you. Those offshore waters are thick with sharks. The villages are constantly losing trepang di-vers."

"Well, I made it. But do you know, within a week I very nearly made the dastardly mistake of trusting another such fellow? I just barely escaped having the same horrible thing happen all over again. So do you see, Captain, why I could not bring myself to trust you?" She wanted to be able to see his face just now and she could not. "Now that I know you, I realize I could have come to you with my story and you would have given me passage to England freely and clearly. But I didn't know you then. And those other experiences—I was trapped, I was half a world away from home, I was sick to death of tropics and exotic places. And you needed a cabin boy." The telling wearied her. She drew her knees up and rested her arms and chin on them.

"As you said, an honorable way home to England. And I refused to believe you." A hand bumped against her arm. The fingertips ran down it to find her hand. He took it in his. His own hands were warm again. "I apologize for not ac-cepting you. I had no evidence to distrust you and you claimed your honor. I should have respected that."

"Why? As you so rightly pointed out on that greensward,

my refusal to explain anything to you made me suspect, and quite reasonably so. I see that now. But then, I just couldn't bring myself to tell you all this. I mean, intimacy with Joshua—well, it was natural and proper. But Abram Sykes soiled me. He defiled me. I was afraid—"

"But if he victimized you, it certainly wasn't your fault."

"Regardless of the blame, I am defiled all the same, don't you see? And I was afraid of what you would think of me. It matters to me just as much now—maybe even more—but somehow now I can talk about it, and then I couldn't. Do you suppose it's because of this darkness and we can't see each other, or because the danger above is so imminent?"

"I have no idea." His hand released hers and traveled back up her arm. It cupped around her head just behind her ear. The fingers pushed up into her short hair. "I immensely admire your gift for plunging ahead and burning your bridges behind you. You got this idea to pose as a cabin boy and less than twelve hours later, you're sitting in my cabin with your story and your plan all worked out. And you couldn't very well go back to being Erica once you whacked your hair off like this, could you?"

"It wasn't all courage, believe me. I cried for two solid hours after cutting off my hair. You're right, though; I'm impetuous. Always have been. Marrying Joshua like that—impulse. Decide this, decide that. So it breeds trouble? Well, charge on forward and find some more trouble. I suppose if you want to spend a life out adventuring, it's a handy character trait to have. But it does cause wear and tear and pain."

"All the same I should have more of that impulsiveness. I'm too cautious, too slow at times."

"And I must learn to take better heed; you're really a

very good model for me. I must think things through more carefully.''

''Are you familiar with the difference between the Gospels of Luke and John?''

''I, well, I presume they were written by two different men.''

''True.'' He chuckled again. ''They complement each other, dovetail their information. Except for a few passages, they talk about different things altogether. We complement each other that same way.''

She leaned her head into his hand. ''I never thought of that. It's quite true. You're steady; I bob about like your Mr. Fisher—''

''Not as bad as Fisher.''

''No one bounds through life like Fisher. You know what I mean. You're very proper and careful, and it is glaringly obvious that I am not. And as you say, there's that matter of impulsiveness.''

''Impulsiveness. Yes.'' He was drawing her head over toward his voice. It took her a moment to realize what was coming. Somehow she could easily picture Maude kissing just any old pair of lips that wandered into range, but this was different, very different. This was the straight captain and the cabin boy/girl who perplexed him so, his partner in a quite probably lethal dilemma. Surely—

Their lips met softly; his aim in this pitch dark was extraordinary. He wrapped around her, encased her in the strength of his arms. She melted against him and let him pull her in close and tight. Her body, her spirit, all her senses hung suspended in the blackness. How long did she float in this happy oblivion, and did he float as happily? In due time his lips left hers, brushed along her cheek and kissed her neck. His hand pressed her head against his shoulder.

She murmured, "Excellent impulse. You learn quickly."

"Not impulse. That was very carefully considered." Those gentle fingertips massaged her neck behind her ear. She would have liked to rest her hand on the nape of his neck, but she feared she might accidentally bump a sore spot.

She snuggled deeper in against him. "How long considered?"

"I told you. When I came back aboard after leaving you yesterday, I sat down in my chair, remember? And the cabin felt empty. It wasn't the lack of, ah—" Ever gentlemanly, the voice stumbled, groped for words. "The lack of a man-woman relationship. Maude Harrington was available up on the quarterdeck if I were so inclined. It wasn't the absence of someone to set the table. Any man aboard could be pressed to that service. And the emptiness was complete. Hollow. Almost frightening. It took me a while to realize just why the emptiness was there, and that you hadn't really left my mind since the voyage began. As Eric—or as Erica—you were all I thought about."

"Puppy love," she lied. "You'll get over it."

"At my age?" He paused. "Why did you come back? The truth, please. The real reason."

"Because I had determined on my long walk out to some rocky little point southeast of town that I, too, am a victim of whatever this may be."

"Why did you stay and fight? They didn't want you."

"I don't know."

"You could have run, found help—"

"Help came—a couple of gendarmes—but they decided not to get involved. Besides, I couldn't just watch them drag you off not knowing—I mean—oh, I don't know what I mean. I suppose it would have simplified matters considerably had I broken away. Impulse again."

"You should have saved yourself."

"Well, I didn't. But I have a better suggestion. Let's both save ourselves now. Any ideas?"

He took a breath. A little chuckle rumbled down inside. It exploded as a cheery, lilting laugh. The fingertips moved up to her ear and both his hands cupped around her head. He held her face as if he were looking at her eye-to-eye. Incredibly, they locked eyes in spite of the blackness; her imagination filled the dearth.

His voice was warm and happy with the pleasure of her. He had forgiven her past—he didn't have to say so—and her heart sang. "Do I have ideas! However dark it may be, my Lord is watching over my shoulder all the same, and I know He wouldn't approve of the idea I favor most. Besides, the faster we look for a way out, the better our chances are."

"A way out? Two hatches and the companionway, and I'm positive someone unsavory and ominous will be waiting on the other side of any of those exits."

"Possibly. We'll go exploring." He hauled himself by degrees to his feet. He rocked a bit, unsteady, so she pressed close—to keep him upright, of course.

"Exploring, eh? More adventuring. Very well, you take the lead. It all looks alike here to me." He was leaning on her, however slightly, and it gave her great pleasure to be of help. "The fruit of all this: I'm learning quite a bit about adventuring. Do you know, for example, that its charm is almost all in whom you do the adventuring with?"

"I concur. Absolutely."

She wanted him to kiss her one more time before they went plunging off through the blackness, but she was too short to initiate it. If they were to kiss, he would have to bend down to her.

And he did.

CHAPTER 16

Java Sea, Afternoon, June 19, 1851

Most of the Anglo seamen Fisher knew looked askance at native vessels—considered them crude and haphazard arrangements of ill-fitting boards. The appearance of these weathered craft would tend to foster that impression; Fisher could see that. And at one time he, too, had looked down his nose at Oriental watercraft. But now that he was serving aboard one, he was altogether impressed. Efficiency, maneuverability, comfort—this lorcha had all the best qualities of any seaworthy vessel. And now that he knew, he could see those qualities in the ponderous junks and feathery outriggers as well.

Perhaps, should this Maude Harrington/Gideon/*Arachne* business fall apart completely, he might simply stay on with Hwang Ahn here. There were far worse things in life than plying the South Seas in a worthy vessel. Moreover, now that he was surrounded with no one else, all these Orientals didn't bother him at all. Professionally speaking, these seamen were as skilled as any Fisher had ever known, and that included DuPres. He even enjoyed his turn at the tiller.

142

Why, he hadn't handled a tiller since he sailed dories off Knockadoon Head when he was just a wee shaver.

Thoughts of his own pleasant childhood reminded him of Gideon. In a way Fisher was glad he had never married. This one lad was a heavy responsibility. Imagine the onus of a whole houseful of tads, not to mention the little wife to keep happy.

And what if he accidentally yoked himself to someone like Maude Harrington? Ah, a splendid body had Maude Harrington, and without doubt she knew how to use it for purposes of pleasure. But if the Dutchman were only half speaking the truth (and the Dutchman's whole mien suggested truth spoken in anguish), Maude was cutting out simply because she had tired of responsibility. If Fisher ever married he would marry the responsibility along with the woman, and Maude apparently didn't feel that way. How could he know for certain that the girl he wed was ready to stick it out? Marriage was an incredibly complex contract, to be undertaken only by a wise man capable of seeing into the future.

Yet even without marriage, Fisher found himself responsible for the lad Gideon. The responsibility had been thrust upon him, but he would discharge it cheerfully. He would protect the child and succor him, and if need be, see him safely into his teens when he would go off on his own. All in all, it was a rather pleasant prospect, this matter of having someone so bright and precocious and affectionate utterly dependent upon you. Unlike marriage, this responsibility was limited and its end visible.

The glaring sunlight must have washed some sky color into the water; it rendered the sky pallid and the water a deep, rich blue.

Hwang wandered foreward and a few minutes later came wandering aft again. He stopped by Fisher's side at the larboard rail. He smiled and pointed off abeam. A large bird, from this distance no more than a thick white streak, soared a few feet above the swells. As they watched, it dipped in closer, swooped gracefully, heeled starboard, coasted in so close on the lorcha's wake that Fisher could see the color of its eye. The wings must span three yards at least.

Hwang leaned out to watch it better. "Remind me, please, its name in English."

"Albatross. 'All wings and appetite,' me mate McGovern calls it."

"Al, yes. Albatross. Good fortune, they say."

"Aye, so I 'ear."

"And like good fortune, very rare. I have only seen one or two my whole life at sea."

"Rare in these seas, aye. If ye sail much down in the roaring forties ye'll see 'em aplenty. They seem to like blustery weather and choppy seas. In fact, meself cannae recall ever seeing one this deep up into the tropics before."

"Indeed. An omen of luck, then, perhaps, to come this far north."

Fisher grinned. "Wouldn't it be grand."

Albatross. Lady Luck. No—divine providence, Captain Bricker would insist. Fisher was not about to argue the fine points of difference, if any. Right now he could use the ministrations of albatross, Lady Luck and God—all three.

Total darkness renders everything exactly alike—no beauty or ugliness, no shades of gray. Erica pondered the equalizing effect of pitch black as she gripped the tail of the captain's jacket. He was groping his way along the belly of this ship. Apparently he had some notion where they were; at least, so far they hadn't bumped into anything insurmountable.

"Now where are we?" she asked.

144

"Still moving aft. I can't say exactly because I don't know how long she is or where we were to start with."

"How do you know we're moving aft?"

The jacket went slack. He had stopped. "Let's sit a minute." He plopped down rather hard.

She settled close beside him. "Are you certain you're all right?"

"I'm fine. Remember when we were standing on the foredeck that morning and I was weaving the yarn about Nereids?"

"The highlights of my life. And since it's totally dark you can't tell from my face that I'm telling you the absolute truth."

"I believe you. From now on I'll believe you when you say something—within reason, of course."

"Until that moment I was convinced that all the men in the whole world—except the vicar, maybe—were exactly alike. Vermin. You changed my life with those Nereids of yours."

He was quiet a moment. Apparently he had decided not to comment on that. "The wind then was to our backs—actually more off to one side. That was unusual. The prevailing winds quarter from the other direction this time of year. We were enjoying a rare occurrence when the wind was right for a change."

"Very well. So?"

"Assuming that fair breeze wouldn't last, and the wind is, therefore, pretty much what it usually is; and assuming this vessel is bound for Singapore—"

"A likely assumption with Maude up there in the stern cabin."

"Precisely. Then feel the ship's cant, how she's tilting."

Erica scooted her legs around to her right a bit. "I think now I'm facing downhill, so to speak."

An arm reached out and bumped her legs. "That's right. So from the tilt of the ship and knowing the way the wind usually blows, I'm assuming that aft is to my present left, your right."

She sighed. "It must take a lifetime to learn all these things."

"Now here's why we're moving aft. Feel the litter on the deck?"

"Litter?" She patted the floor beside her. She felt occasional bits and chips, something soft like bark.

"And the last clue, smell the air."

"Smells like wet wood. This entire hold smells like it. I assumed that's normal since it's built of wet wood."

"This vessel has been hauling teak logs lately—the bark chips, the distinctive teak smell. If so, it may be fitted with sternports for lading the long lengths of lumber."

"What are sternports?"

"Little doors at the very back under the transom."

"Doors!" Erica beamed so happily she half expected the hold to light up. "A way out! Open the doors to admit some light, fashion a raft and launch it well after dark. Excuse my lack of chivalry, but we leave the fair Maude to whatever fate awaits her."

"Maude. I don't see how we can possibly rescue Maude unless they decide to toss her down here with us. You didn't happen to see the name of this vessel as you were brought on."

"No. I'm not even sure it has a name. Oh, surely it must."

"Well, let's find the sternports first." He moved, rustling in the darkness.

She stood up and bumped into him. "Sternports do stay in one place, don't they? Don't sneak about?"

"Of c—now what are you getting at?"

146

"Well, if we needn't rush right over and leap on them, perhaps there's time for one short kiss."

He laughed. The artificial wall he had constructed between proper ladies and proper gentlemen was gone, gone to the last brick. Was it the darkness, or the point she made that she and Eric were the same, or simply their present danger? Would the wall reerect itself once they were safe somewhere, should that happen at all? She didn't want to lose this oneness again. She pressed against him as his lips brushed her cheek, their aim slightly off, but quickly found together.

She must shore up this fragile unity now, the more so, if by chance, Maude would indeed be sent down here. Maude was much less resistible than Erica; in a contest of physical attractiveness, Erica would lose. From what she knew of men, there was one certain means of buying a man's temporary allegiance. The captain's God would just have to turn His back a few minutes, that's all. Erica was not voluptuous like Maude, in fact hardly endowed at all, but she pressed her small body hard against Bricker's.

He gripped her shoulders and broke the kiss off instantly. "Don't." He whispered hoarsely. "Please don't. I'm closer to the brink than you know."

She let a sob slip out. *I'm so unattractive I can't even seduce a man who claims to like me!* She sniffled. Maude could have done it. She would have purchased or bribed his devotion somehow. She had both the gift and the equipment to take what she wanted from men. The tears edged up and over and out.

"I'm afraid."

"I don't blame you." He wrapped his powerful arms around her. "Try not to be. We'll get out of this."

"It's not this I'm afraid of."

His hands moved up to cup around her head again. His

147

thumbs stretched out forward and wiped the tears from the corners of her eyes. He was looking into her face again, through the blackness. "What are you afraid of—that I'll forget about you?"

She nodded in his hands.

"Don't ever be afraid of that, Erica. Don't ever be afraid of that."

"Even if Maude steps back in—or someone like her? There are inordinate numbers of Maudes, you know—multitudes and multitudes of them."

"And there is only one Erica. Which is more desirable, one unique diamond or many common pebbles?"

There was silence in the blackness, long moments of it. Then he was kissing her, at once firm and pliant, soft and fierce. The tears dispersed. No, she would not have to offend his God by pulling any of the little tricks in a Maude-like repertoire. She felt suddenly light-headed—from the kiss? Or from the giddy revelation that Erica was being loved for what she was—herself—and not because she happened to be a convenient female?

He relaxed his ardent bearhug eventually, topped off with a final little peck, and found her hand in the blackness. There was no more hanging onto coattails. He led her by the hand as they worked their way aft in silence.

They bumped into a stack of crates and struggled together, moving them aside; Erica was sweating profusely by the time they worked through the pile. She heard the gentle thunk of his hands against—against what sounded like thick wood. He grunted with exertion. Metal creaked on metal and set her teeth on edge. A white vertical line streaked the darkness. Hinges groaned and brilliant searing white sunlight blasted in. It overwhelmed her eyes. She clapped her hands to her face and peeked by degrees through her fingers.

She knew she must not speak loudly, for human ears were

just a few yards overhead. Yet she wanted to scream joyously and jump up and down. He pushed the door open a little further and hung onto the frame as he leaned out. After studying the situation overhead, he pulled himself back in.

He kept his voice low. "The counter's deep enough that they can't see us, even if the door here swings out wide."

Raucous voices drifted down from above. Someone laughed.

Erica's eyes were adjusting now. She pointed out to sea. Far astern a blob of white canvas and a dark cutwater followed them. "Look at that."

He studied. He squinted. He grinned broadly. "Guess who!"

"Arachne? But how—? That means we're saved!"

"Not yet. See our shadow on the water? The mizzen? This ship is larger than she and full-rigged. They don't have to work hard at all to outdistance her. She's not catching up; I'll wager she's falling behind."

He sat on the frame leaning out, staring at the side. She stuck her head out, too. He seemed to be studying the rudder. He looked up. She looked up. The shadowy hull of a little boat swayed back and forth above their heads. Nothing suggested itself to her, but obviously he was scheming.

He sat back and leaned his head against the frame. She had forgotten he must still have a dreadful headache. She sat down on the frame across from him, half in the hold and half in the open air of freedom. Their wake gurgled and boiled beside her.

He was studying her thoughtfully. "You're not strong enough to muscle a jolly boat around by yourself. But you are impetuous and clever—"

"I believe we established at least half of that."

"Can you dream up some story to get above decks, back here to the quarterdeck? There's a light dinghy above our heads, the captain's boat. It hands by light line from davits, out over the water. Can you cut it free?"

"It drops in the water, we both hop in and we sail away." Her face was alight with the dawning of his plan.

"That's half of it. While you're up there I'll be down here finding something to jam their rudder with. If I can skew the rudder, *Arachne* will walk right up to us." He sat up straight. "The Lord has been with us this far. Let's do our best and pray the continuation of His favor."

Religion again. She raised a finger. "Listen."

He frowned, expecting trouble.

She pointed to the wake. "Nereids. Would they be singing this cheerfully if we were doomed to fail?"

He was going to say one thing, apparently, and decided upon another. "Sure they would. They're just happy to see sunshine on your face again. Bunch of aquatic romantics down there."

She leaned over suddenly and gave him a quick kiss, the sort of fast peck married folks give each other as one is going out the door. She hopped down off the frame, started away, stopped, and turned to him. "I love you." It was whispered, it was sung. She ran because she could not simply walk. She grinned irrepressibly because she could not feel serious.

She remembered in one of the vicar's homilies that he read from the Bible about charity. He claimed charity was a translation for the Greek (or was it Latin?) word for *total love*. He said it was ever patient, kind, forgiving, and giving; he said love was never rude, irritable, or selfish. *What a terrible burden love places upon one,* she had thought at the time. That showed how little she had known about it. Right now she wanted to be all those things to Travis Bricker and more.

The last shaft of light disappeared. Again she was moving

150

through complete blackness. But all the blackness was on the outside. Inside, her heart glowed bright as midday.

How long could she remain in this state of euphoria before the pirates above their heads killed one or both of them? She would leave that problem to Captain Bricker's God and bask in this heady new delight as long as possible.

She pressed on through the darkness, groping—

CHAPTER 17

Java Sea, Late afternoon, June 19, 1851

It occurred to Erica as she stumbled through the blackness that she had not the least idea what she was doing. She had never actually been in the hold of a ship before. Was she on the deck just below the surface deck? Was she deeper still? How was she to tell when she passed a hatch? With the covers on the hatches they were all just as black as the rest of the hold. She stopped and peered all about. It was as if she were under a thick blanket. She continued on.

Her searching hands rapped into something immovable. She patted it. It seemed to be a wall. No, on ships they were bulwarks, not walls. Or was it bulkheads? She was no sailor. She groped along toward her left, a random direction. Something whacked her on the ear. She reached for it and felt—a ladder. She scrambled up.

The hatch at the top was covered but she removed the lid easily enough. The hatch opened onto another deck, equally black. She remembered to put the hatch cover back on. She didn't want to fall into it during her gropings and wanderings.

She explored what seemed a long time before she found another ladder. She climbed it and tried to push the cover aside. It wouldn't budge. She felt around the inside edges. Whatever latched it held it from the outside. She knocked on it. She thumped on it. She pulled off her shoe and pounded its heel upon it.

Long moments dragged by. She had started to pound again when she heard strange scratching noises. The cover lifted. Blaring sunlight dumped into her eyes.

"Ho. It's the lad." One of the three ugliest men Erica had ever looked upon peered down at her. The other two stood near him.

"Might I come up, sir? Please? He's dead. My captain's died and its frightening down there." She sniffled and ran her sleeve across her nose.

The blackguard stared at her a moment, reached down, and yanked her up by one arm. She stood by obediently as he fastened the cover down again.

His breath was foul. "So 'e's dead, eh? 'E was nae good color when we put 'im down there. Suspected as much. Be ye sure?"

"Wouldn't be standing here if he weren't. I can't abide touching dead people, and he's cooling off already." She shuddered.

The three traded glances.

Erica took a deep breath and straightened. "Might I sign on as cabin boy? I'm very good at serving, sir."

All three laughed.

"Don't 'ave much trouble switchin' loyalties, 'ave ye."

"Ships is all about alike, sir."

"Come along. Got a thing to show ye. 'Sides, the old man's got questions ye may 'ave answers for." He gave her a shove in the right direction.

She stumbled and jogged ahead, her shoe still in her

hand. She would put it back on when she found the time. *So far, so good.* Captain Bricker's God was holding them in continual favor. She almost smiled at herself. Just listen to her! She was talking about his God much the same way he did, as if his God were a very real presence. She almost slowed down, thinking about it: *What if Captain Bricker's God were really a living entity right here on the Java Sea with us? We've gotten this far safely, haven't we?* That was some evidence of His helping hand, at least.

She had no time to think further. She got an additional prod up the quarterdeck steps. Three or four scruffy sorts were lolling against the taffrail, passing a jug amongst them. *Arachne* seemed smaller now in the distance. The captain was right; she was losing ground.

The ugly seaman dragged her up before a man with a blue rose tattooed on his cheek.

"'E says Bricker's dead.''

"'E did, now. And 'ow does 'e know that?''
girl. She glanced past the dinghy's davits, not permitting
sexton back in Shropshire. He plants 'em all the time.''

Ugly chortled. "'E wants a sign on with us.''

The tattooed one grunted and grabbed Erica's chin. He twisted her face aside, looking at the dried tear-streaks. "Who wants a crybaby? Not me.''

"M' father might plant 'em, but I don't like 'em all the same, sir. Not sittin' next to 'em as they gets cold, and no daylight.'' She tried to sulk as a boy would sulk, not as a girl. She glanced past the dinghy's davits, not permitting her eyes to rest long on any one spot. She scanned the array of sabers and belt knives and dirks which ringed her. She certainly had her choice of cutting tools, if only she could grab one.

Tattoo-cheek raised his telescope to his eye. "Reckernize that vessel out there, lad?''

"No, sir. They all look alike. Specially at that distance."

"Hit's y'r own *Arachne* out to rescue the captain. Losin' way. I don' mind sayin', though, that she's a few knots faster'n a bark-rigged vessel like 'er ought be." He turned to Erica. "The lady in my cabin back there claimed to be Mrs. Bricker. That'd be the captain's wife. Be they married all legal-like? The Dutchman'll wanna know."

Erica shrugged. "Don' know, sir. I wasn't ring-bearer at no wedding, is all I know."

There was a general display of merriment, no doubt encouraged by that jug. Erica seemed to be playing it right so far.

"Well, lad, was they bunkin' in the same cabin?"

Now how should she answer that one? She was trying to think of something innocuous and noncommittal that would protect the captain's good name, should it be spread abroad. As it turned out, she didn't need an answer.

Behind them the helmsman yelped. "M' hand's broke!" The great wheel moved all by itself as the fellow exploded with a string of oaths.

The deck tipped starboard high and port low—slowly, gracefully, inexorably. A couple of the seamen, their equilibrium already altered by inebriation, tumbled downhill to the far port railing. The jug shattered against a rail post and two men moaned simultaneously.

Tattoo-cheek was sliding away from her. Erica reached out and snatched the closest hilt at hand, a small saber at his side. She jumped up on the taffrail, surprised that no one thus far had noticed her. She glanced over her shoulder. Those sailors still on their feet had dived for the great wheel. Three or four of them were tugging at it, trying to swing it back aright.

Down at the port railing, at least four men were tumbled together into a tangle of churning arms and legs, all

155

generating an overbearing quantity of foul words.

Erica swung out, hacking at the davit line in front of her. Two swipes parted it. The dinghy's stern dropped from sight. She side-stepped, crablike, downhill along the taffrail. The dinghy hung forlornly by its pointy nose. She slashed out at the remaining line.

The line parted and the dinghy disappeared just as Ugly realized what she was doing. He charged at her with a snarling oath, and Yellow Teeth came boiling up the quarterdeck steps. She swung the saber at Ugly, not really wishing to do him harm. He howled and fell back, but she didn't pause to see what she had done or not done. She took one big step to the top of the taffrail and leapt out into empty air.

She hung suspended in space for an inordinately long time—seconds and seconds, it seemed—before the sea slammed into her. Instantly frigid salty water engulfed her, pierced her clothes and drenched her nose and ears. She remembered now that she had forgotten to take a deep breath. Her nose and eyes burned. She began to kick wildly, furiously, blindly. It occurred to her also that she had never learned how to swim. Her only real experience in water (save for that horrifying night when she escaped the clutches of Abram Sykes) was paddling about in the culvert near the parish. This was not the same thing at all; there was no mucky, gooey, safe bottom to touch.

Erica's view of life from water level was frighteningly different from that just a few inches above waterline. Even when she surfaced she felt submerged. She couldn't get her head far enough out of the water to see properly. She was choking and coughing too hard to kick.

From nowhere—from behind—an iron-hard arm clamped around her neck. Her head was locked back and she was being dragged through the water by forces far stronger than she. She gripped the sleeve for dear life. A gray something loomed just inside her peripheral vision. She reached out, flailing, and grasped a protruding ring. The gray something bobbed on the swell, but seemed otherwise solid. The arm released her and disappeared, so she clung to the ring. A strong hand gripped her back; she could not fall away.

Another spate of coughing partially cleared her lungs.

He was beside her, right beside her. "All right?"

She nodded vigorously and coughed again. "Oh, no! Our boat! It landed butter-side-down! I did it wrong!" She stared at the captain, panic-stricken.

He was grinning. He looked immensely, totally happy with her. "You did it right. In fact, you just achieved the impossible. What did you ever say to those . . ."

Someone from the ship was firing a gun at them. The little boat jerked as slugs struck its other side. Well beyond them, the ship was still arching in a smooth curve to port. Even as she watched, the sails spilled and the ship skidded to a casual halt. Its canvas flapped uselessly as it wallowed.

"Better right this thing before they put a longboat down and come after us. Hold on right there." He slapped the wood.

She gripped the rough wooden gunwale and asked no questions. He worked his way around to somewhere else. Suddenly the wood ripped out of her hands. She grabbed it again, panicky. The boat was bobbing low in the water and right side up.

His voice called, "Climb in over the transom there."

She had no idea whether this was the transom, but this was where he had left her. She hauled herself up, squirmed and wiggled, kicked and tumbled into the boat. It was nearly as full of water as was the ocean. She struggled to sitting on the forward seat.

An oar came flying up over the side, then another. She looked toward the pirates' ship. It wallowed, its masts marking huge, lazy arcs. The brigands were indeed lowering a longboat just as the captain feared, but they seemed to be having considerable difficulty. The launch project was not coming along well at all; the longboat jerked about, remaining virtually in place.

The captain's head appeared above the transom; disappeared momentarily; came shooting straight up. He tucked and landed in the bilge. The little boat tipped side to side perilously, its gunwales nearly awash. He came up grinning and plopped onto the center seat. "Frankly, I never dreamt we'd get this far this smoothly."

"Smoothly? Our little boat is nearly at shark level and I almost drowned."

"Minor problems."

"And wasn't this supposed to be the plan?"

"Cooking up an idea as wild as this and actually accomplishing it are two different things. Here. Bail some of this." He pulled his jacket off and folded it roughly. He scooped bilge once in demonstration, and tossed her the coat. He clunked the oars into their locks in one swift motion, dipped one oar deep and pulled with the other. The little boat pivoted in place. He leaned on the oars and started them moving sluggishly away from the pirate ship, toward *Arachne*. He grunted. "A boat full of water hates to move."

Erica scooped madly. She seemed to be making some progress. They had a good three inches of freeboard out there now. They bobbed toward *Arachne*, up swells and down. More gunshots cracked from the ship.

"You asked her name. Did you see a name?"

He shook his head. He was sweating. "No. Apparently they aren't telling."

She paused from bailing, winded, to look back at their kidnappers. The pirates must have abandoned their idea of putting down that longboat, possibly because it now dangled from one davit, useless.

"Stand up and wave my coat. Be careful; don't tip us."

She looked toward *Arachne*. She stood up, teetery, and flung his jacket back and forth joyously. *Arachne* was coming straight toward them under a heavy press of sail. The gleaming canvas billowed bright, drum-taut. Oh my, she was a lovely ship. Erica looked back again. The pirate vessel didn't even have the same colors of canvas in its sails. They were patchworks of white and yellow.

The captain glanced over his shoulder. "They see us. Sit before we capsize."

Erica clung to the rough wooden gunwales, too relieved and happy to do much bailing. *Arachne* was close enough now that she could see the frothy cutwater. Nereids must be scattering in all directions!

Nereids. They were silent out here among the smooth swells. Or were they? As the water drained from her brimming ears, she could hear more than just the loudest noises. The Nereids were here, accompanying this tiny craft as it undulated across their world. She could hear them now as she listened carefully, soft and tender, whispering.

CHAPTER 18

Java Sea, Late afternoon, June 19, 1851

Fisher took in a deep breath of clear and sparkling sea air. *"Una boneeta día, verdad?"*

"Sí. Muy bone-eeta." Gideon seemed to have resigned himself to Fisher's tortured Portuguese-*cum*-Spanish. He only snickered a little at it now and then. In fact the clever lad, almost equally fluent in Spanish, tempered his own good Portuguese to make it sound more like Fisher's fumbling polyglot. This brilliant lad was indeed a pleasure to be responsible for.

Fisher and Gideon walked the length of the lorcha's deck from stern to stem. Fisher scooped the lad up and perched him on the forecastle roof. They were now far enough removed from Oriental ears that they could murmur *sotto voce* in English awhile and actually communicate.

Fisher cuffed the boy affectionately. "Y're doing splendidly, lad. Now listen quick 'ere. We may call at Macassar in the next few days to pick up supplies. Soon as we get anywhere near a dock, y'r to jump ship and disappear."

"What about you?"

"Ye needn't worry about old Fisher. Meself can talk me way clear of any foul weather. Ye just make sure ye escape clean."

"Whatever you say." Gideon sprawled on his stomach to look over the side as the water boiled up around their hull. "The Old Man ever tell you 'bout Nereids, Fisher?"

"I've 'eard of Calypso and 'er lot. 'E's got a book about mythology in 'is quarters, ye know. Ye should read it sometime. Exciting stuff."

"Yeah. Soon's we find him."

"Aye, lad. Soon as we find 'im." Fisher grimaced.

Gideon knew how big the Pacific Ocean was. There was no fooling the lad, no lulling him into thinking everything was hunky-dory. Chances varied from slim to impossible that they could successfully reach New Zealand and the *Arachne*. Gideon knew pirates when he saw them, too, and sensed at least to some extent their present predicament.

Fisher realized that sooner or later he would talk himself into some pickle he could not talk himself back out of. But Gideon's safety and well-being were quite another matter. If Fisher lived or died by virtue of his wits, it was Fisher alone. This innocent child must not die for Fisher's flaws. Responsibility has its limits. Perhaps Fisher ought to bare all to some trusted seaman here and extract from him a promise that Gideon would be spared and given haven. Hwang, the crook, was not the person to approach thus. In fact, in this boatload of crooks there was not one Fisher could begin to trust. He could only hope they would raise Macassar before Hwang became suspicious. Gideon was quick enough to do well if only he could escape.

The afternoon was starting to wane. Fisher noticed that this was the first day that the boy was not excessively tired by this hour. He was waxing stronger. What would he say when he encountered the usurper Eric? No matter just yet—he was nowhere near strong enough to take up his duties. There would be plenty of time for them to work some arrangement. Difficult choice, though—as much as Fisher liked Gideon, he really liked young Eric immensely, also. Eric was bigger than Gideon. Perhaps they could shunt him into some more responsible position.

Fisher smiled at himself. Talk about your optimistic outlook! Here he was making long-range plans concerning Gideon and *Arachne* and Bricker and Eric and—*that's the spirit, Fish, old top! Keep a bright eye to the future!*

One of the lookouts shouted something only the heathen Chinese could understand. Fisher peered at the horizon and saw nothing.

"Alla." Gideon pointed almost dead ahead. Sure enough, a white speck floated on the line twixt sea and sky. They glanced at each other. Both knew the other's thoughts even without words, for they shared the same wish. Might it by some impossible chance be *Arachne?* Fisher knew it couldn't be; *Arachne* was headed east beyond Australia.

Fisher patted Gideon's knee. *"El sitt-o 'ere-o, Chico."* He wandered aft. Here came Hwang with a big brass-bound telescope. "Might I take a peek through that when y're through?"

"With my pleasure." Hwang walked over to the rail, studied the approaching ship briefly, and handed the glass to Fisher.

"Lovely piece. European, eh? German?" Fisher wondered what poor packet the blackguards lifted it from, but would not be tactful to mention such thoughts aloud. Fisher spoke loudly enough for Gideon to hear easily. "I see—ah. Aye, there's a cro'jack. Full rigged. And no colors. Know 'er, Hwang?" Full rigged. It was not a bark—not *Arachne*.

Hwang retrieved his glass and studied the ship further. The question was no longer of interest to Fisher. He had

162

identified who she was not, and that was identification enough. Hwang purred, "Ahhh." Apparently he enjoyed the challenge of identifying random vessels of no consequence. His first mate came wandering up and they exchanged a few words concerning the approaching ship. Hwang handed his glass back to Fisher. "Do you see anything unusual about her?"

"Unusual?" Fisher peered through the glass. " 'Er canvas is brought 'ome fair; mainsail's goose-winged; seems to be making the most of the breeze. I see naething remarkable about 'er. What does y'rself see?"

"Examine her canvas."

"Looks good. Spencer and flying jib look to be sewn up of two different lots of canvas—top's yellowish, bottom's whitish." He lowered the glass, frowning. "Many's the time a sailmaker 'as to stitch together two unlike bolts. That be not so unusual."

"If you inspect that gentleman's sail lockers, you will find his spencers and flying jibs to be of like manufacture."

"That be 'is mark, y'r saying. Ah, then ye do know the vessel."

"The record shows the Norwegian ship *Stavanger* ran aground near Port Moresby, and two weeks afterward the derelict was broken up during a typhoon. That is the record. In truth, she ran aground but her captain and all but two of the crew foolishly abandoned her, thinking her beyond salvage. Her present master used the high storm tides to help lift her free and made her his own. To speak with strictness it was an act of piracy; he dispatched the two crewmen in order to claim her."

"I see. But the captain feared to make an issue of it, lest 'is own poor judgment come to light. So 'e wrote 'er off as lost aground."

"Exactly."

"Then I venture she's seaworthy and then some."

"Her reputation is for speed." Did Hwang's even voice carry a slight tinge of irony, perhaps of bitterness?

"May'ap y've locked 'orns with 'er master."

Hwang frowned, puzzled.

Fisher translated. "Ye've 'ad a fight or two with 'im. Or per'aps a race ye lost."

Hwang chuckled. "Astute, Fisher, and better spoken than you realize. We are rivals, not enemies. But races? Many. He takes great pride in the speed of his ship, and in the fierceness of his crew. He and I are engaged in the same occupation. We pursue the same trade. He considers anyone of Oriental race, ah—" Hwang waved a hand, "beneath his level of excellence; beneath any European's. He feels this particularly so in our mutual field of endeavor, or pursuit of trade." Hwang glanced at Fisher. "On rare occasion, this pursuit transgresses the boundaries of law. I look at it as a necessary risk when reaching for high profits. He considers himself above the law. You see the difference.

"I follow ye. Met a few of them sorts meself, 'oo views the Irish in a similar dim light. And y're itching to do 'im one better, but so far 'is own ship 'as outpaced y'r lorcha. Of which, as ye say, the bloke be insufferably proud."

"Insufferably. One day, rest assured, I shall surpass him. I shall obtain a prize that he might consider his. Perhaps I shall even bring him to his haughty knees, and with no small degree of glee. My men are able, my vessel strong."

The erstwhile *Stavanger* was swift indeed. Already it had approached closely enough that Fisher needed no glass to see details. But he raised the telescope to his eye anyway, just to be certain of what he saw.

"Ah, Hwang. That albatross wasn't just luck for meself. 'Ere may be y'r chance to sail circles around 'er. Looky there, will ye." He pointed.

The distant ship had altered course. She was turning slowly, majestically, to port, veering away from the lorcha. Should she veer just a few degrees more without resetting her sails she'd lose way completely. Aye, and there she went. The canvas luffed and spilled; she wallowed helpless in the swells.

Hwang very nearly smiled. "An unusual maneuver in open sea. You are knowledgeable about such craft. A problem, perhaps?"

"I'd say something in 'er rudder. A steering chain parted, or some pintles sheared. Something of that sort's crippled 'er rudder, prevents 'er from 'olding 'er rudder true."

Hwang nodded. A little half-lift raised the corners of his mouth. He spoke in Chinese and the mate at Fisher's left laughed out loud. Hwang purred, "I believe we shall approach her closely enough to express our condolences. How unfortunate we are in too much the hurry to actually remain at her side and render aid in this time of, of—crisis." He shouted nasal orders to his crew and to the man at the tiller. With hearty good cheer, sailors scurried all over. Apparently the rivalry was not only between captains. The lorcha leaned slightly astarboard.

Gideon came flying down off the forecastle. "Fisher! Look! There's a ship a-chasing, her, Fisher, coming on hard! It's her, too! I just know it's her!" He ran up to Fisher and snatched the glass from his hand. He dashed to the rail and peered through the telescope, his arms nearly too short to manage it. "It's her, Fisher! *Arachne!* I'd know her anywhere!"

Hwang's slanted eyes narrowed to a dangerous squint. "Portuguese?"

"I'm, ah, teaching the lad a bit of English. Right smart little shaver, ain't 'e? Catches on so fast."

Gideon had forgotten everything in the world save the joy

of seeing home. "It's her all right. There's the black splash down her foreroyal, where Halloran dropped that bucket of tar!"

A sharp point pricked Fisher's back just above the kidney area. He jumped, startled, then steeled himself. It was the mate's dagger. Instantly another pirate materialized behind him.

Hwang stood just behind his elbow now. "You have not been completely honest with us, Fisher, though we have long suspected as much. Perhaps it is best we discuss right now the true connections between you, this humble lad with the gift for foreign tongues, and the bark *Arachne*."

CHAPTER 19

Early evening, June 19, 1851

The scaling apparatus, a rope ladder, came snaking down the vast, flat black impenetrable, unscalable fortress wall of the ship's flank. Erica stood up and snatched at it. She caught it on the backswing.

"Straight up. There you go." The captain was hanging onto a light line as their little dinghy sloshed beside the slippery, towering hull of *Arachne*.

She clambered up the ladder. Half a dozen strong hands grabbed her arms and the seat of her pants and hauled her over the rail. Men were grinning and laughing all around her.

"Here he comes. Easy, lads!"

The captain's head appeared above the rail. He almost fell back, but the gaggle of willing hands dragged him inboard. His feet hit the deck, his knees buckled. For some reason Erica glanced at McGovern, the stoic. The dour Scot's face was twisted in pain concern, as if this were a favorite son rather than a master. The captain straightened and leaned back against the rail. He glanced around. His eyes rested on Erica.

She smiled and waved, an "I'm-fine" sort of gesture.

The captain rubbed his face wearily. "Break out the guns. Maude's still aboard there."

McGovern patted the pistol in his belt. "We're ahead of ye."

"You? With a gun?"

McGovern shrugged. "We were fixing to bring ye off by force of arms if need be. Don't know how ye did it, but we're mightily pleased."

Yes. Erica looked around. They were indeed mightily pleased, every jack here. Travis Bricker was more to them than a mere sailing master.

"It's the Lord's providence and none of our own doing." He inhaled deeply. Even from her distance, Erica could see he was looking better. "Range in closer. It won't take them long to figure how their rudder fouled, but it should take them awhile to right it. We have a few minutes left to work."

"Aye." Mr. McGovern started to turn but Halloran was already off shouting orders and calling to the helm. The first mate peered closely at the side of his captain's head. "Mmph. Found blood at the site, but we were hoping it weren't yours. See we were wrong."

"How did you know to pursue us?"

"Fifteen minutes after ye left, the lady insisted on going ashore to buy cosmetics. By the time I sent DuPres and Lampeter after 'er, she was gone. They found a parcel lying in the street—talcum and foofoo things. And, lo, here's a string of vermilion blotches here and there down the street. Led DuPres straight to the wharf and the very berth. He saw y'r vessel moving out into channel and we were underway and giving chase in no time atall. From the tracks around the fight we knew ye were with 'em, but we didn't realize about young Eric."

"You kept up with her well."

"She's fast, but we've the breeze to our quarter, the lady's best side. Lucky we kept as close as we did."

"Luck, Mr. McGovern?"

The Scot forgot himself and smiled. "Providence. My mistake. But having this particular old girl beneath our feet didn't hurt, ye know. Ah, she loves t' fly! Here's Edward! Splendid. Soon as we saw ye commandeer the dinghy, I sent him to brew coffee." McGovern relieved the towheaded young man of two steaming coffee mugs. He handed one to the captain. "Here ye go. This'll put ye to rights quick enough." He looked all around. "Ah, Eric. There ye be. This one's for y'rself, lad."

Erica crossed and took it, gratefully. "Thank-you, sir!" Though the tropical heat was drying her soaked clothes, it cooled her so quickly she was almost shivering.

"And how did yerself fare in that fight? Did ye get any good licks atall or did ye stand by and watch?"

"Got kicked in the side. I'm fine, sir."

"Strip y'r shirt off there. Let's have a look."

Erica clamped her elbows against her sides so tightly she almost spilled her coffee. "Oh, I'm sure it's fine, sir. Ask the captain. He already—ah—he, uh—questioned me closely about it. I'm fine. Really."

McGovern nodded. "Let one of us know if ye've trouble breathing or if the pain hangs on for days."

The captain's jacket was bobbing about in that dinghy yet, somewhere in the Pacific. His light sweater must have been cooling him off also as it dried. He wrapped both hands around the hot coffee mug. "We heard shooting from both sides. Anyone hurt?"

"Nay, they were loading that deck gun on their forecastle. DuPres managed to squeeze off a couple good ones with your Sharps rifle. Discouraged 'em from hanging around their cannon."

From aloft a lookout called, "That batten-sail craft, sir. She's ranging close in; might be trouble."

The captain frowned, puzzled.

"One of those trim little flat-bottoms the Portuguese built for snuffing pirates."

"A lorcha?"

"Aye, that's it. We spotted 'er some time ago but thought nothing of it." McGovern was peering off beyond the tangle of shrouds beside him. "Arrgh. It's right here among us. Don't smugglers own most of 'em now?"

"Never heard of one in the hands of an honest seaman." The captain leaned out a little, watching it.

Erica strained on tiptoe at the rail beside him. It was a rather pretty little boat if you didn't mind that business about dishonest seamen. Its hull was earthy red; its cabins fore and aft, a cheerful yellow. The little deck house in the middle, somewhat discolored, probably had started out white. She could distinguish faces there. It seemed to be an exclusively Oriental crew.

The captain sipped at his coffee. "Mr. McGovern, we know she's not with us. And if they left Macassar in a hurry, it's doubtful she would be with them. But if she did mean to join them we can't fight two crews to a standstill. Maude may need help, but I won't risk the lives of my own crew to get her out of there."

"We're willing to go after her. Our own decision. In fact we all agreed on it before ever ye came off their vessel. Unanimous."

"I know you're willing, and I appreciate it, but—"

"Your bullhorn, sir?" Edward wedged between Erica and the captain.

Arachne had swung about. They were now broadside the nameless ship and not a hundred yards away. Erica could make out some facial features. Ugly was among them, so she must not have hurt him too badly.

"Very good, Edward. Mr. McGovern, try to keep their vessel between us and the lorcha until we know more about her."

"Aye, sir." McGovern trotted off.

"Edward, I want every free hand aboard to line up along our rail with a gun easily visible. You might mock rifle barrels up with some mop handles, too. We want an impressive show of force."

"Got it, sir!" The towhead grinned and ran off.

Halloran filled the spot Edward vacated before Erica could move back in. "Don't suppose ye'd find this 'andy, sir." He extended the big ungainly Paterson.

"Thank-you, Mr. Halloran." The captain lifted his bullhorn to his mouth. "Ahoy the ship." He separated each word carefully. "Surrender Maude Harrington unharmed and we'll let you go your way. No complaint, no retaliation."

A laugh and some sort of expletive floated across from the crippled ship.

Halloran rubbed his hands together gleefully. "A demonstration, aye, sir?" He turned grinning to Erica. "DuPres's a good sharpshooter, but the Old Man here's better. A joy to watch."

The captain had wedged his coffee mug between two deadeye lanyards by his shoulder. He raised his pistol with both hands. "The swells aren't making this any easier."

His gun blammed and spit smoke. Erica flinched. The ship's port running light exploded in a little burst of red glass. The crew crouched lower behind their gunwale.

Captain Bricker brought his bullhorn up. "Maude Harrington, gentlemen, or I pot-shoot skulls instead of lanterns."

Erica whispered, "Would you really?"

"No, but they don't know that. As Paul wrote to Titus, to the pure everything is pure, but the defiled think in defiled ways. They assume I'm cut of the same bolt they are, and they wouldn't hesitate to blow us all out of the water if DuPres would let them get at their cannon."

There he was, quoting Scripture again.

Halloran grinned even wider. "I do believe they're considering it. And that lorcha's hove to. Just sitting there. Wonder what she wants."

"All we can do is wait and watch."

Up and down the rail, half of *Arachne's* crew stood sober and ready, brandishing guns and mop handles of all descriptions.

Erica had some time to think, it would seem. She folded her arms on the rail and rested her chin on them. Item: *The captain's relationship with his crew was most revealing*. He held them in great esteem and they, him. Moreover the captain not only cared about them but trusted them utterly. He trusted his God even more. The men beneath him were trustworthy; it was logical his God was also. Esteem probably followed the same lines.

Item: *I may not know this God personally but the captain very obviously does*. And because he did, it followed that his God was knowable on a personal basis. It further followed—if he could, she could.

Item: *The captain resisted my clumsy advances not because he did not like me—his kiss proved otherwise—but because he did not want to offend his God*. Not once did he mention fear of punishment by some harsh Jehovah. Erica did not doubt that an all-powerful God could wreak whatever havoc He wished on those who displeased Him, but the captain placed fear secondary. Most of all he wanted to please his Lord. This idea was new to her.

Item: *The captain is firmly convinced his God provided*

172

our way out of the pirates' clutches. He certainly was a better judge of such matters than she. And now that she thought about it, they had indeed achieved the impossible. He had single-handedly crippled their ship. She had successfully fooled a crew of wily connivers long enough to steal a boat out from under their noses. Ridiculous. Impossible. It couldn't happen. Yet here they both stood safe.

She mused awhile over all the little odds and ends of evidence she had picked up since meeting this man, evidences of his relationship with the Almighty. Her mind seemed almost as muddled as the time she had tried to work out the nature of God. But something within her had changed. She was now less concerned with knowing about God and more concerned with knowing God. She knew Joshua, like the captain, had known God. But he had never really asked her about her own convictions and she had never volunteered, lest she spoil her chance to go adventuring.

The man farthest aft called, "They've righted their rudder, sir. It's swinging free to both sides."

The captain raised his gun again and steadied it two-handed against the deadeye by his ear. Hunched low and skulking, the crewmen across the way were moving to their stations.

"She's gonna run for it, sir!"

The captain's gun blammed blue smoke again. Erica knew it was coming, but flinched anyway. Aboard the other ship a voice yelped and a belaying pin shattered at the main fiferail. The line it held swung free.

The captain raised his sights somewhat and squeezed off another one. A heavy block dropped to deck, bringing several lines with it. From somewhere around the forecastle, DuPres's rifle cracked. More fiferail lines fell loose.

"Mr. McGovern! Bring us athwart hawse of her; give her

173

the choice of veering off or ramming us. We'll engage her rigging if we must.''

''What about the lorcha, sir?''

''She hasn't raised a finger to help them so far. Let's take the chance she's neutral and waiting to prey on the victor. They may not—''

A minor cannon blasted. A blue-gray cloud of gunsmoke lifted off the lorcha's deck. From aloft the ship with no name, the far upper fourth of the middle mast creaked. It tipped slowly, with excruciating grace. Casually, languidly, it creaked more and began its topple. Upside down it came, still with that easy grace. It plunged like a sword through the orderly web of lines, parting a few of them, fouling others. It stopped, hopelessly tangled, ten feet above the deck. It bobbed up and down.

A faint voice, barely audible and clearly Irish, came over from beyond the stricken vessel. ''Put Maude over the side, laddies, or we bring y'r mizzen down next.''

Erica frowned. ''That sounds like Fisher.''

Mr. McGovern pressed in close beside her. ''What's an Irishman doing aboard a batten-sail? They ship with their own, the Chinese.''

A flurry of blue appeared near the ship's stern. They were bringing Maude Harrington to the rail.

''Would ye look at that! Shall I block 'em off or give 'em a moment?''

''Give them the moment. But let's make sure that's really Maude and not a Trojan Horse.''

A whitish sort of doughnut ring was jammed down over the blue. Suddenly the whole blue billow came flying over the rail. Maude wore lace pantaloons under her crinolines. She hit the water shrieking in strident soprano. Erica recognized a couple of the words as being part of her basic repertoire.

The two men spoke simultaneously. "It's Maude."

The captain nodded. "Order arms, gentlemen. We said we'd let them go. Lower a boat and bring her aboard."

Arachne's crewmen made their guns a little less visible—reluctantly, it seemed to Erica. One by one the sails on the other ship—those few with rigging intact—spread and filled. Like an aged old crone, the ship dragged herself forward.

Her master leaned against his taffrail. Erica could make out the blue tattoo only because she knew it was there. His voice was easily audible without a bullhorn. "I'll not forget this, Bricker!" He turned toward the lorcha. "Nor you, Hwang!"

Erica could see a Chinaman aboard the lorcha bow in perfect courtesy. She could also see now why the vessel with no name might consider itself outgunned. Not only were the *Arachne* crewmen well-armed and irate (and demonstrably good shots), the Chinese boat sported two menacing deck guns, both level point-blank on the ship. The struggling vessel was making a little better way now.

Arachne's longboat splacked into the water. Erica peered over the side to watch it. Halloran and another seaman took to the oars. It pulled away toward Maude.

Mr. McGovern gasped, totally startled, totally incredulous. "Captain, do ye ken any Chinese sailors with red hair?"

"Red ha—you don't suppose he managed to—praise the Lord!"

Fisher moved to stand at the lorcha's rail beside her master. A dark head appeared beside him, barely rail high.

"And the bairn," breathed McGovern. "He's got the lad with him. Providence, captain? Nay, a miracle. Nothing short of a miracle. If I was an infidel a minute ago, I'd be a believer now."

Erica stared wide-eyed at Mr. McGovern, and at her captain. It was not just what these two had just said, it was the intensity with which they believed every word. McGovern did indeed acknowledge a miracle. And her captain was indeed praising his God for an abundant providence. Erica remembered vaguely the vicar saying that one must approach God in prayer by first making confession. *General confession: Almighty God, Father of our Lord Jesus Christ, Maker of all things, Judge of all men; We acknowledge and bewail our manifold sins and wickedness, Which we, from time to time most grievously have committed, By thought, word and deed, Against thy Divine Majesty, Provoking most justly thy wrath and indignation against us. . . .* No. This would not do. She could recite the *Book of Common Prayer* end to end, and she had never once thought what she was saying. She must pray sincerely now, not deliver a recitation. Later she would study what she had been saying all these years.

She had all manner of things to confess, but what weighed heaviest was that sinful attempt to seduce the captain, God's faithful servant. What hurt most was that she had so lightly and glibly set out to offend God. She must put that first in her confession; already she vowed to do her best to avoid future offense.

The oarsmen hauled Maude indelicately up over the transom. She sat on the floor of the longboat, a sorry, sagging, soggy blue pile.

The lorcha bobbed in closer. Its two deck guns were now trained upon *Arachne.*

The captain's voice rumbled beside her, strong and steady, reassuring. "If it comes to a firefight, lads, shoot for the gunners on their cannon and stay clear of Fisher and Gideon amidships."

Erica would confess later. Pressed by a vague but insistent urgency she simply asked whoever was listening that the God of Abraham, Isaac, Jacob, Joshua Rice and Travis Bricker be her God as well. She would do as His Son Jesus commanded because He wanted her to. And she certainly remembered well enough Jesus's own words, "I am the Way and the Truth and the Life. No one comes to the Father except by Me." Or however that line went. She would try from here on to please God, not in fear of punishment (though knowing full well it lurked as a possibility) but because she wanted to please Him. She would follow her captain's example in that regard. And in her confession, when she got it worked out, she would mention her hard-heartedness. She was sorry about that, too. If it took a miracle to bring her to God, well, that's what it took. Still she should not have been so recalcitrant.

What was involved in this commitment? She did not know yet. But once she set her mind to something, she followed through. She always followed through. The captain would help her. Scripture would help most. She had determined her course now, and she would stay upon it. For some reason she could not fathom, this latest decision pleased her immensely.

The longboat clunked against *Arachne's* flank.

From the lorcha, Fisher called, "Captain! Before ye ship 'er aboard—"

Captain Bricker leaned over the side. "Hold a moment, lads. Aye, Fisher?"

"Captain, Hwang 'ere is considering ye might wish to swap Gideon and me for the fair lass in y'r longboat there."

Maude tilted her head up. The curls, once saucy, were now bedraggled ropes. "You surely wouldn't consider it!"

Fisher called, "She's married, captain. Mrs. Franz Bilderdijk."

"He's lying!" she snapped. "Can't you see he's lying to

save his skin? He has to say that to convince you to trade."

"No, Miss Harrington," said the captain quietly. "Fisher can prevaricate instantly. He can lie like a barge at anchor. But in this situation he does not—he would not—lie to me."

Fisher's voice floated in. "She's the mother of three little ones. Got it straight from the Dutchman's mouth."

"That's not true!" Her voice was rising. "You mustn't believe that lying knave. He'll say anything—anything at all—to get off that stinking boat. You know that. Don't you dare listen to him!"

The captain was looking at her. That was all, just looking. She averted her eyes suddenly and turned on Halloran. "You don't believe him, do you? Please! Don't let them do it!"

The captain's voice was so gentle and sad Erica had to fight the impulse to hold his hand in sympathy. "I'm very sorry, lady. Your marriage is a commitment in which I cannot interfere. Mr. Halloran, make the trade."

Grimly, sadly, Halloran nodded. The longboat pulled away.

Maude shrieked a string of invectives that turned the air as blue as her soppy dress.

Aboard the lorcha Fisher and Hwang were bowing politely to each other. Fisher appeared to be paying him some money. They bowed again, then shook hands. Fisher laid his arm across the little boy's shoulder. Then they climbed out over the side and hand-over-handed down a light line into Halloran's boat. Fisher tied the rope around the violently resistant Miss Harrington and called "'Aul away, lads." By the time Maude's feet touched deck, Halloran was halfway home.

The lorcha's main sail tilted suddenly and caught the breeze just right. Like a dipping petrel she heeled, showed a bit of her flat bottom, and turned on the wind, bound for Singapore.

Erica pitied Maude in a way. *Was she truly married?* If the captain believed Fisher, so would Erica. Still, if Maude felt so very trapped that she would go to these lengths to escape her marriage—whether right or wrong—well, Erica did feel sorry for her. Maude had lost either way.

Halloran's longboat shouldered affectionately against the bulging wall of *Arachne*. Fisher set Gideon on his shoulders and climbed the rope ladder. Eager hands scooped the little boy over the rail; he was smothered instantly in hugs. Grinning and laughing, he greeted each man by name. A precocious lad, this—he seemed not at all intimidated by the noise and attention. Here came even the Chinese cook to greet the prodigals.

She stood back away from the cluster of exuberant well-wishers. She was not a part of this. She was not one of them. Oddly enough, she did not really want to be a part of it. Jealousy? The captain's arms were wrapped around the lad now and the boy was inquiring anxiously about the spectacular marks on the captain's head. Erica, as Eric, had enjoyed exactly that sort of wholesome intimacy. Was she jealous of a scrawny stripling? *Yes.*

McGovern dispatched sailors hither and yon. *Arachne* ceased wallowing as her sails filled one by one. She lurched and pressed forward, under way again.

Fisher overflowed with words. "I thought we were zonkered for sure. But then ye pealed out on y'r bull'orn there, telling the blackguards to 'and over Miss 'Arrington. 'Aha!' cries I to Hwang. 'She's aboard there. 'Elp convince 'em to give 'er up and ye can 'ave the pleasure of turning 'er in for the reward. All yours. What ye say?' And Hwang bought it. So if ye 'adn't used y'r bull'orn, we'd not known Maude was available for the plucking. That Hwang, Captain—'e

179

'as 'is own set of ethics, but 'e takes great care to follow 'em. A gentleman 'e is—a proper gentleman."

The captain scooped Gideon into his arms and he and Fisher walked to the stern cabin. Erica fell in behind them.

The verbal torrent flowed relentlessly on. "Soon's we figured Maude was obtainable we worked the swap. The reward for 'er is considerable, ye know. Considerable. Hwang was dee-lighted, I aver. Sez 'e always wanted to pull one out from under that particular rascal. I suspect *Arachne's* guns 'elped considerably in changing the blackguard's mind for 'im. Ye looked formidable there with y'r lineup on the rail. Where did ye get all the extra rifles?"

Erica hopped ahead and held the door for them.

"The mop locker. What's the vessel's name? We should keep an eye out for her."

"*Stavanger* before she wrecked. She's a salvage; don't know 'er name under 'er present larcenous ownership."

The captain set Gideon on his feet. "You look like you were pulled through the hawse-pipes feet first. You're over-due for a nap, scamp. You'll have the guest quarters until you're strong enough to take over your duties. Off you go."

The boy's feet dragged he was so tired. He paused in the doorway to what was once Maude's bailiwick. "Sure good to be home. Thank-you, sir." He disappeared inside. The door closed. The bunk ropes creaked.

"Mr. Fisher, give Mr. McGovern a hand, please. We may not raise New Zealand in time to earn that cargo, but we can make a first-class attempt at it."

"A little extra canvas maybe, sir? Short watches and long rations?"

"See to it, Mr. Fisher." The captain smiled. "Glad you're back."

Fisher left, words still tumbling out of him.

The cabin was stuffy. Erica pulled open the transom windows. The one to port stuck halfway. She wanted the soft air, the cooling breeze. But mostly she wanted to listen. So the cabin boy was back. The ship was functioning fully. They didn't need Erica now. The captain's world was righted; the people he held dear surrounded him again. Did he still need Erica at all? Or was what happened in that oppressive hold merely a product of the moment, of the temptation, of the disorienting effects of his injury? She sat down with her ear by the opened window. Did that bunch of aquatic romantics down there sing any hope for her at all?

. . . AND THE ADVENTURE'S END

A bit later, June 19, 1851

Arachne was stretching out to her full speed now, drawing the most from her canvas. She heeled only slightly aport, charged ahead with power and purpose. Her wake, rather skimpy before, was now a firm, smooth vee. Erica's side ached where she had been kicked. Her backside was still stiff when she flexed the muscles there. And she felt incredibly weary. Her eyelids drooped. She laid her head against the window sash and let the breeze stroke her face. The Nereids were putting her to sleep.

She raised her head. She could feel him standing near her. She could actually feel his presence, a curious sensation. He was simply looking at her, thinking apparently, with his thumbs hooked into the corners of his pockets.

What should she say? She didn't know. Her head grew too heavy. She leaned back against the sash again and watched the rippling wales of their wake. "I'm glad your friends are back safe. The people on this ship fit together and there seems to be something out of joint when you're not all together." She tilted her head around to look at him squarely. "I'm sure I'll be looking for excitement eventually. But I've had quite enough of adventuring for a while. Peace and quiet has an inviting ring to it now."

"Yes, it certainly does." Was the captain at loose ends? He shifted his weight from one foot to the other and folded his arms, a sophisticated adult version of a shy schoolboy called upon to recite. "Maude doesn't have the presence of mind to lay a trail of vermilion powder. Was it you?"

"Yes. But you can see that I wasn't going to pipe up and say so. It would sound as if—I mean—you know."

"I know." Silence. Then: "Uh, how long was your hair before you cut it?"

She twisted a little and held her hand flat near her tailbone. She smiled and shrugged. "It'll grow fast."

"I hope so. The Scripture says a woman's long hair is her glory. If all of it was the color of what you have left, glorious is an understatement."

"Thank-you." She felt her cheeks get warm. Had she thought of him as a schoolboy? Anyone would swear by her behavior that she was still in the little parish grammar school. She came around with her back to the water in order to sit and look up at him comfortably. "Do you know? I didn't find that irritating at all."

"Find what irritating?"

"Your reference to Scripture. It used to annoy me. Religion, religion, religion. I, ah, apparently have had quite a profound change of heart, more so than I had suspected. I hope that doesn't sound maudlin, but—"

"Maudlin! It sounds wonderful!"

"I'm glad you think so. I haven't had time to really sit down and work it out inside my head. I'd like to do that first. Organize a little."

"In other words, you'd rather not talk religion now."

She smiled. "Every time I try to convince myself you're

nothing but another of those callous, uncaring men, you surprise me with your sensitivity."

"I have to sit down." He walked across the room and picked up his favorite chair. He half dragged it over and plunked it down three feet from her. He melted into it. His legs and arms drooped, flaccid, in all directions. His day had been rougher by far than hers. Wouldn't he rather shut himself in his quarters and sleep the next eighteen hours away? She was not about to suggest it. Selfishly, she did not want him to go. She said nothing.

He shifted in his chair and leaned on one elbow. "Forgive my staring. It's not polite, I know. Now that I look at you—I mean, really look at you—I don't understand how I could possibly have mistaken you for a boy. Your face, your form—there's nothing masculine anywhere. Not even a hint."

She chewed her lip a moment. A small light dawned. "Perhaps it's because you wanted to. A lady you must hold in abeyance. But as a boy I was, ah, more immediate. Talk, joke, act normal, one might say. I mean—there are, you know, things your head thinks about down so deep you don't realize it. Like that vermilion powder business. My head thought it out, but it was two blocks before I realized what I was doing. Do you understand what I mean? Here was a person whose company you enjoyed; and you could enjoy it much more comfortably if that person was a boy. You needn't be so infernally and constantly polite, you see. So guarded." She frowned. "Does any of this make sense at all? I'm so tired I can't think clearly."

"It makes very good sense."

She was staring past him now, looking at a rain-wet wharf in Singapore at dusk. "That first night, when you brought little Gideon ashore—it was the eyes. I'm certain it was the eyes. They were so large and they said so much.

184

Not to say the rest of you is not attractive, understand. You see, I had promised myself no more men—to forget men. Enter a convent or something—preferably not a cloistered order, should I wish to take up adventuring again. Men were scum. And then—'' She tried to snap her fingers. They wouldn't snap. "There you were. Am I speaking out of turn?''

"What's your feeling about men now?''

"They're still scum, all but one. Only one. With him I could be happy. All the rest can stand by and watch me walk in through the convent gate.'' She sat up straighter. "Why speak in veiled terms? I refer to you. That first day, when I was still Eric to you—it was so very pleasant, for both of us. Loose and free and open. I beg you, please let us go back to that. If you really try, I'm sure you can treat Eric like—like Eric. I so want to stay on here, to recover that—that—that feeling. It's the thing I want most.''

He shook his head. "It would never work. You can't roll time back like that. You might call it a time of innocence. I was ignorant of who you were and you were still innocent of any deep feelings about me. But now I know, and you know, and we can't erase what we know. It's changed, Erica. Permanently.''

She sagged back and let her eyes fall shut. They felt hot. She certainly hoped she would not make a fool of herself by weeping or by any other such schoolgirlish behavior. "You're right, I suppose. Still, it destroys the only thing I want.''

"Is it the only thing you want?''

She opened her eyes. "I don't know what I want, except to regain that special relationship and hold onto it. You know, where there was no wall of propriety. I don't mean something improper. Not something your God would frown upon.'' She paused. "Actually, it's our God now, to be more accurate. Anyway, I mean when we—"

"I understand." He cut her off. The sun crinkles were starting to crowd together a little. It was not quite a smile, not yet, but his face had a sly twinkle about it. "When a ship loses way she loses helm. That is, to steer a ship and go where you want to go, you must keep her moving forward. It's an excellent rule of life as well. We can't go back, but we can move forward."

The door opened at the other end. Mr. McGovern stepped out of sunlight into gloom and crossed to the captain's chair. "Arrgh. Y're just sitting here. Ye ought to be closeted in y'r quarters, getting some rest. Ye look like death in a thundermug."

The sun crinkles bunched a little tighter. The expression on his face suggested that he knew something Erica didn't. Erica knew he knew something Mr. McGovern didn't. "Mr. McGovern, I think I shall make you captain for a day. Two days. No, a week. Captain for a week."

"I accept the temporary promotion with pleasure, sir. Ye can do nicely with a week's rest. Ye deserve it. Indeed, 'twill take the better part of a fortnight just to rid y'rself completely of that headache, I'll wager."

The captain was smiling at Erica. Would she ever be able to bring herself to call him Travis? She could not imagine it. He was her captain. He was speaking not to his first mate but to her. "I believe you know, Eric, that while on the high seas, captains are empowered to perform marriages. But I suggest it would be distasteful, if not illegal, for a captain to officiate his own nuptials. Does that answer your question?"

"Aye, sir. It surely does."

"Mr. McGovern, pull up a chair and sit down here, please. I have a story for you that will jar your teeth loose and curl your toes."

Erica found herself grinning so widely her cheeks were getting tired. His proposal was, to say the least, unusual. But then, even that was fitting; this whole relationship was unusual beginning to end. End? Not yet. Beginning. Just beginning. She drew a foot up onto the sill (the one still without a shoe; she could not for the life of her remember when she parted company with her shoe), crossed her arms across her knee, and buried her mouth in the crook of an elbow, lest she accidentally give something away. What she wanted most was to leap up and kiss her captain roundly and extensively, but that, of course, would spoil his grand revelation. And the laughter in his eyes told her he was preparing an absolutely lovely surprise for the dour Scotsman.

Were her eyes laughing, also? He had locked onto them with his own and through them was bespeaking love across the silence. And he was grinning now, irrepressibly. They both reveled in their secret these last few moments before it became common knowledge.

Suspiciously the good Scotsman clunked his chair down nearly between them. "And now what's going on here, ye two magpies? Y're acting like knaves of hearts, the both of ye."

"Mr. McGovern, you'll remember I told you how Eric's sister asked me to consider him—"

She sat back and watched out the open window. The sun perched at such an angle now that their wake danced with white and yellow flecks of brilliant light. Did Nereids wear jewels in their hair? Of course the captain was relinquishing his position for a week. Who wants the burden of command on what is essentially a honeymoon cruise?

His voice was rolling on, nearing the dramatic moment. She listened with one ear. At just the right time she would turn, smile sweetly, and wink at the astonished Mr.

McGovern. You see? They fit together so well they could pull a splendid little prank with no rehearsal. And yes, she could listen to that voice for a lifetime. She waited for the perfect moment, and with her other ear listened to the bubbling wake, the breaking whitecaps, the Nereids' song.

ABOUT THE AUTHOR

Little did SANDY DENGLER and her husband know what was coming when they cashed three books of trading stamps in on a model kit of the clipper *Cutty Sark*. Over a dozen ship models now sit about their home in Ashford, Washington, and their two daughters—one, a marine biologist major; the other, a sailing enthusiast—have come to share their parents' pleasure for things nautical.

Sandy's zeal for history, geography, and the sea is tempered by a strong tendency toward seasickness. Ships are romantic so long as they are firmly attached to a dock!

A Letter To Our Readers

Dear Reader:

Pioneering is an exhilarating experience, filled with opportunities for exploring new frontiers. The Zondervan Corporation is proud to be the first major publisher to launch a series of inspirational romances designed to inspire and uplift as well as to provide wholesome entertainment. In order that we might better contribute to your reading enjoyment, we would appreciate your taking a few minutes to respond to the following questions and return to:

Anne Severance, Editor
Serenade/Saga Books
749 Templeton Drive
Nashville, Tennessee   37205

1. Did you enjoy reading SONG OF THE NEREIDS?

☐ Very much. I would like to see more books by this author!
☐ Moderately
☐ I would have enjoyed it more if _____

2. Where did you purchase this book? _____

3. What influenced your decision to purchase this book?

☐ Cover   ☐ Back cover copy
☐ Title   ☐ Friends
☐ Publicity   ☐ Other _____

4. Please rate the following elements (from 1 to 10):

☐ Heroine   ☐ Plot
☐ Hero   ☐ Inspirational theme
☐ Setting   ☐ Secondary characters

5. Which settings do you prefer?

_____   _____

_____   _____

6. What are some inspirational themes you would like to see treated in future Serenade books?

_____   _____

_____   _____

7. Would you be interested in reading other Serenade/ Serenata or Serenade/Saga Books?

☐ Very interested
☐ Moderately interested
☐ Not interested

8. Please indicate your age range:

☐ Under 18   ☐ 25–34   ☐ 46–55
☐ 18–24   ☐ 35–45   ☐ Over 55

9. Would you be interested in a Serenade book club? If so, please give us your name and address:

Name _____

Occupation _____

Address _____

City _____ State _____ Zip _____

Serenade Saga Books are inspirational romances in historical settings, designed to bring you a joyful, heart-lifting reading experience.

Other Serenade Saga books available in your local bookstore: